"WHAT WE DECIDE TODAY IS NO MORE AND NO LESS THAN THE FATE OF THE WORLD..."

★

The Yankee Stadium crowd remained silent, perhaps aware that they were in the presence of the Holy.

The voice continued. "If we cease our virtuous contribution, the world will continue its slide into the abyss. If, on the other hand, you, Dexter, can convince us that the world is redeemable, then we will redouble our endeavors and take up the struggle with renewed vigor. You will be given the chance to defend humanity, by offering your life story as testament of the worth of the world."

"Wait!" I cried. "If I can't convince you, are you going to kill all the good, innocent people along with the sinners?"

"Ah, the cry of Abraham. Wilt thou also destroy the righteous with the wicked?" The voice commanded, "Begin..."

★   ★   ★

PRAISE FOR STEPHEN BILLIAS
*THE AMERICAN BOOK OF THE DEAD**

★

"A wonderfully bizarre, charmingly antic first novel by a talent to watch."
—**Harlan Ellison**

"Funny, moving, and enlightening."
—**Robert Swigart, author of**
The Book of Revelations

"Billias reads like Aesop rewritten by Tom Robbins."

"A funny, original, and nuclear issue."

*Recommended readi

Also by Stephen Billias

The American Book
of the Dead

Published by
POPULAR LIBRARY

ATTENTION: SCHOOLS AND CORPORATIONS

POPULAR LIBRARY books are available at quantity discounts with
bulk purchase for educational, business, or sales promotional use.
For information, please write to SPECIAL SALES DEPARTMENT,
POPULAR LIBRARY, 666 FIFTH AVENUE, NEW YORK, N Y 10103

ARE THERE POPULAR LIBRARY BOOKS
YOU WANT BUT CANNOT FIND IN YOUR LOCAL STORES?

You can get any POPULAR LIBRARY title in print. Simply send title and
retail price, plus 50¢ per order and 50¢ per copy to cover mailing and
handling costs for each book desired. New York State and California
residents add applicable sales tax. Enclose check or money order only,
no cash please, to POPULAR LIBRARY, P. O. BOX 690, NEW YORK,
N Y 10019

the Quest for the 36

STEPHEN BILLIAS

POPULAR LIBRARY

An Imprint of Warner Books, Inc.

A Warner Communications Company

POPULAR LIBRARY EDITION

Copyright © 1988 by Stephen Billias
All rights reserved.

Popular Library®, the fanciful P design, and Questar® are
registered trademarks of Warner Books, Inc.

Excerpts from *Words Like Arrows* compiled by Shirley Kumove,
copyright © 1984 by University of Toronto Press, Schocken
Books, published by Pantheon Books, a Division of Random
House, Inc. Reprinted by permission of the publisher.

*Excerpt from the Talmud (B. Yoma 69b), as quoted by Raphael
Patai, *Gates to the Old City* (New York: Avon Books, 1980).
Reprinted by permission.

Cover illustration by Richard Hescox

Popular Library books are published by
Warner Books, Inc.
666 Fifth Avenue
New York, N.Y. 10103

 A Warner Communications Company

Printed in the United States of America

First Printing: October, 1988

10 9 8 7 6 5 4 3 2 1

for my father
George Athan Billias
who taught me to love Justice

Contents

1

The Yearning

My name is Dexter Sinister. Mr. Right Left. Yeah, when it came to naming me, my father was a real comedian. Why couldn't he have given me an ordinary handle like Joe Sinister? Instead, I've spent my life in search of balance. Naturally this quest has flung me on the wildest swings of the pendulum.

You might say that I lead two lives: one as a talent agent for variety shows, the other as—what shall I call myself —a cosmic detective. Like Harry Houdini in the twenties, I expose false prophets, defrock phony TV evangelists, unmask religious charlatans of all kinds. It's my hobby. Some wise early investments have provided me with the means to indulge these two whims and a predilection for travel. Like Houdini, who was driven by the hope of speaking to his dead mother, and thus refused to accept fakery, I too want the truth, the true word. So, like Harry, I collect lunatic fringe religions, hoping to stumble across the real thing.

I was on my way in from Far Rockaway when a tall black man stepped into the car at a station somewhere in Brooklyn. The A train thundered through tunnels of darkness. Inside, our fluorescent temple of graffiti gleamed and shook. The young man wore a white robe and a white knitted yarmulke, and he carried under his arm a stack of magazines. He proceeded to hawk his wares in a loud voice: "Brothers and sisters, *Sholom allah h'a allu*. Why do I say to you, *'Sholom allah h'a allu'*? Because it is written in the Koran, the Torah, and the Book of Revelation that this is the ancient greeting of the tribal brothers. I am of the Black Sons of Abraham. We believe in the united wisdom of the original twelve. Why twelve?—twelve tribes of Israel. Jesus had twelve disciples. That is why.

"We teach self-sufficiency and skills, carpentry, plumbing, electrical, because if you work for the white devil you are dependent on him, but if you work for yourself you are self-sufficient—"

There were maybe twenty-five people on the train. In this city the religious magazine salesman might have pitched his wares a hundred, a thousand times to bored and jaded, stupefied and noise-numbed New Yorkers, but on this night something amazing happened as we hurtled through caverns of cement-covered bedrock.

Before he could get to his pitch for money, the Muslim/Jewish/Christian splinter in his yarmulke and caftan was confronted by two bearded young men. They were lugging an enormous floor-cleaning machine, a buffer or polisher of some sort, with brass handles on each end. The thing (which sat at their feet) must have weighed at least a hundred and fifty pounds. I wondered briefly how they got it through, over, or under the turnstile, but then the debate was on and I could only listen.

"Get the truth, brother!" one of the two cleaners shouted. He had black hair and a black beard and gold wire-rimmed glasses, and he looked like an anarchist of old. His compatriot had a blond beard and saintly eyes. "Jesus is Lord! Get hip to that." He smirked at his friend and they burst out laughing. Obviously they possessed the truth and they knew it.

"You have enslaved us long enough. White supremists—"

He got no further. A heavyset Latin woman leaped to her feet. "I'm from the Creation Church," she yelled. "Black, white, yellow, brown, we all worship together. You're preaching hate!"

This was not some homogeneous group returning from a religious convention. These were twenty-five random New Yorkers on the A express in from Far Rockaway, past the racetrack, through Euclid and Utica avenues.

Before long there were a half-dozen people verbally fencing and aiming barbed religious thrusts at one another. The Muslim shouted louder than all of them—he'd had the most practice.

"We believe that!" he cried out when someone challenged him to refute a passage in the Bible: "Love one another."

Some on the train turned away or ignored the commotion. Others like myself watched eagerly. A middle-aged black man, his head covered with a porkpie hat and his pants shiny with age and grease, sat facing the white-robed street-preacher but did not look up. I thought he might be disinterested, but then I noticed that the plastic bag he carried was from a religious bookstore.

My heart leaped up and my mind wondered: what is this yearning? The world is a pit, a Times Square phantasmagoria of pimps, whores, muggers, drug dealers, and fences. We have surpassed Rome and Babylon in grandiose

perversity and general immorality. Yet here beneath the
streets of the city, in a filthy subway with riders too poor to
be chauffeured in limousines or to take taxis, with windows and signs coated with the anguished spray-painted
pleas of an unemployable youth, here where the air is as
hot and stinking as the sulfurous fumes of hell, here on the
A train a religious revival was in full swing.

The yearning was as palpable as the humidity, which
was reaching the dew point.

We passed through Borough Hall and Brooklyn Heights
and plunged under the river to the Battery. People got on
and off, some joined the debate, some dropped out. By
now Mr. Three-in-One was winding down. He tried to ask
people for money for his magazines, but the furor he had
started didn't abate so easily. He was beginning to lose
patience with the obnoxious cleaners.

"Make a donation to support the brothers? Make a donation to support the brothers?" He passed down the aisle,
leaving the Latin woman to step into the breach.

"You all are invited to come to the Creation Church,
Sundays at eight and ten, One hundred sixty-first and
Roosevelt up in the Bronx. God's country."

"Make a donation to support the brothers?" Apparently it
was a part of his routine to ask everyone on the train,
regardless of how they reacted to his speech. He approached even those who had ignored him and those who
scoffed. When he reached the floor cleaners, he stopped.

"Make a donation—"

"We don't pay to hear lies. The truth is free!"

"Don't hassle me, you white devils—"

"Oh, now the true color is starting to show."

"If I wasn't with the church, I'd kick your butts—both
of you."

"Ho ho. Give up your soul to Jesus, and you'll turn the
other cheek."

"Up yours, honky assholes." The man in white finally lost his cool. At the next stop he got out without selling a single magazine.

When I was a junior in college, I took a course in religious revivalism in the 1840s, an epoch in American history when a fervor of religious evangelism swept the country. It was said that whole towns would go off after some wild-eyed minister with a vision. It was during this time that Joseph Smith led his followers—the Latterday Saints of Jesus Christ—west to Illinois, through Indian attacks and hostile religious elements, enduring Job-like privations, only to die without reaching the Promised Land.

Could it be that we are in a new era of revivalism? Are the final days at hand? The two young men with their unwieldy cleaning cross to bear would say so.

One would think that after the proselytizer got off the debate would have died down, but instead it accelerated, because he was no longer there to dominate with superior lung power.

The Latina Creationist rummaged in a suitcase-sized handbag for her own handouts. Triumphantly she produced a wadded-up stack of badly mimeographed leaflets. With a dramatic flourish worthy of the flamboyant television evangelists I imagined she watched incessantly, she took up where here predecessor had left off.

"Free leaflets, free bro'sures," she called out, accenting the word on the first syllable. "Get 'em now, save your soul while you can. Creationism is the way and the truth."

As she talked, in my mind's eye I saw the city rising on itself, layer upon layer: electric cables, gas mains, water aqueducts, subway tunnels, then the street, ancient cobblestones covered with layers of asphalt like unshed skins, and then buildings, starting below in sunken piles and concrete foundations, thrusting up through the substructure until they scrape the sky, and inside them and down below in

sewers and subways and on the streets and flying overhead
in jets, everywhere are people yearning, hungering for re-
demption, salvation, relief.

*May the yearners yearn always, every day in every way,
to the last Hare Krishna domine domine son of a gun one
of them,* I thought to myself, and was preparing to get off
at my stop when a Hasidic fellow with long sidelocks and a
round Russian fur cap caught my eye. He too was preparing to get off. Why hadn't he taken part in the debate, I
wondered? Then I noticed that he was gesturing to me.

"Hssst! Hssst!" he sputtered at me, his head bobbing up
and down like a carnival doll's.

"Who, me?" I pantomimed to him, for the train noise
rained down on us like audio fire and brimstone.

"Yes." He gestured, curling and uncurling his finger like
a troll luring me under a bridge.

I approached him. When I drew near enough, he col-
lared me with one hand and pulled my car up to his mouth.

"We need an observer," he said. The train lurched and he
nearly fell on top of me. The doors slid open in herks and
jerks. We tumbled out. "You saw what happened in there."
He gestured to the now emptying subway car that had
been, for a few moments, a church, a talmudic exchange,
an ecclesiastical forum.

"Observer?" I said, confused at his reference. "The incident is over."

"It's only beginning, my friend, only beginning." He
nodded and mumbled some prayer to himself.

"What's that?" I said.

"Kaddish. The prayer for the dead. I must say it continuously now."

"Why?" I asked.

"Because," he hesitated. "First, do you agree to be an
observer?"

"Why?" I repeated.

"Because there will be so many."

"So many dead?"

"Yes."

"Why, what's going to happen?" Now I began to suspect that the rabbinical costume was a getup, not real. I confidently awaited his gloom-and-doom spiel.

"Everything. You name it. War, famine, train wrecks, airline disasters—"

"So what else is new?" I could be as jaded as any New Yorker.

The Hasid shrugged. "Perhaps you are not the man we are looking for, after all. Read the newspapers or watch television. You will see what I mean."

I thought I heard someone call my name behind me. I turned to look and, seeing no one, I turned back. Then an extra-ordinary thing happened. It was one of those moments, surely you have experienced them, when your senses play tricks on you, an unexplainable phenomenon occurs, the world seems magical for an instant. It might be an unaccountable puddle of water on your floor in the morning, or some object that suddenly seemed to have moved from one place to another, or a lost item reappearing where you've looked a hundred times. This time for me it was the rabbi, somehow he was waving to me from the last car of the receding A train, though I was sure I had heard the doors close several seconds before, while we were still in conversation.

I scratched my head as I climbed the stairs to the street, and I tried to cling to the memory of the yearning, but it was fading as if an image from a dream, elusive and insubstantial.

2

The Three-Midget Flash

Still distracted by the incident on the train, and my chance meeting with the mysterious Hasid, I rushed to my office, a space I rented over a porno shop on Eighth Avenue near Times Square.

On a hunch, I hurried up the stairs, raced through my foyer, past some waiting midgets and a man with a black case under his arm, shut the door in their faces, and switched on the television. In the time it had taken me to ride in from my apartment on the beach in Far Rockaway, a 787 superliner had fallen out of the sky with hundreds dead and scores more casualties on the ground. Helicopter shots of the burning jet wreckage were being broadcast to a horrified but unsated public.

The midgets walked in without knocking. In the lead was a feisty-looking little guy in a spandex leotard top with no sleeves, the better to show off his powerful upper body. He was almost all upper body.

"You Dexter Sinister?"

"Yeah, but look, I'm busy—"

"My name's Fred, and this here is Chuckie, Little Bob, Fahey, Smitty, Jake, and Ralphie."

Where's Grumpy and Dopey? I wanted to say, making the common error of confusing midgets with dwarfs, but Fred didn't give me time.

"We're The Spuds. Heard of us?"

"Frankly, no."

"We think we'd fit right in with your agency, Sinister. We want you to book us on the variety tour you're putting together."

"Don't you guys follow the news? Look—"

I pointed, speechless, to the television, which spewed forth gory images of body parts hanging from trees like nightmarish ornaments, with twisted metal bits of fuselage as grotesque tinsel.

"Big deal," the midget spat, with particular emphasis on the *big*, as if it were a dirty word. "Happens every day. But how often does a midget juggling act walk into your office?"

Before I could get out a jibe like "Twice a week," the little fellow jumped up, grabbed me by the collar, and yanked me down to his level. It was the second time in an hour that I'd had that done to me, and I didn't like it.

"Think about it, Sinister. Vaudeville revival is your specialty, right? And when were the glory years for midget jugglers—vaudeville! My daddy played the Palace, the old Howard in Boston, the Bardavon in Poughkeepsie, all the big vaude houses. Me? How am I doing? A television commercial and film extra work, if I'm lucky. But when we heard about you booking a golden-agers vaudeville tour, we rushed right down."

"From where?"

"What's that to you?"

His refusal to give me a straight answer took me by surprise. Why wouldn't they tell me where they were from? Maybe they were escapees from some prison for short people. I didn't know and I didn't care. Reluctantly I switched the TV set off, not before witnessing the third replay of a burning man fleeing from the downed airliner —staggering, falling, rolling in an agony of flames, then lying still, immolated.

"All right, let's see your act," I said to the midgets, hoping to get rid of them as soon as possible. "Five minutes, that's all I got room for in the show for jugglers." The man with the black case under his arm sidled into the room, not so much walking as crabbing his way sideways. "You mind waiting outside?" I said to him. "I have to audition The Spuds here first, but I'll get to you."

"I like juggling," the man said. I noticed that he clutched his case like—like a bomb. Maybe he walked funny because he was all wired up to it. He had a peculiar stare, too, like a greasy Svengali. He hummed to himself when he wasn't looking at you.

"What's in the case?" I asked, being a direct sort of fellow.

"My instrument," the man replied with the calmness of an insane person. I hoped he didn't mean instrument of death or anything like that. I caught a swatch of Dvorak in his soft under-the-breath humming to himself. It made me nervous.

"All right, okay, let's get those balls and clubs and hoops flying," I said, hoping to distract the maniac I was sure was there to kill me, though I knew not why.

"Oh, we don't usually juggle anything like that," the lead midget rejoined.

"Well, what the hell do you juggle?"

"Each other." And they proceeded to do so—the largest four, relatively speaking, divided into two pairs and between them they juggled the three smallest. It was like this—two midgets acted as the left hand, two midgets as the right hand, and three midgets curled up and made like bowling balls. Each of the pairs formed a sort of fireman's carry of their hands and arms, and between them they flung the curled-up three around in the standard three-ball cascade. It was one of the most amazing feats I'd ever witnessed. When they did a three-midget flash, all three balls...er... midgets in the air at once, I almost keeled over.

"You're hired. What do you get for a week?"

"We don't have an agent; they're all crooks. Make us an offer we can't refuse."

"How about two-fifty a man per week. The cruise is going to run six weeks."

"You're on. Come on, boys," Fred said, and the diminutive troupe trailed out of the office in a mass of bulging shoulders, short muscular necks, and oversized heads, all less than four feet off the ground.

"Hey, where are you going? We have to sign contracts and so forth."

"Back next week. We've got business."

They had been gone for maybe twenty seconds before I realized I didn't get a last name for a single one of them; all I had was their first names and the name of their act: The Spuds. I didn't even know which Times Square flophouse they were staying at. I started to run after them, but the man with the case blocked my way.

"I too wish to audition," he said. I detected a trace of Eastern European in his accent, perhaps Czech or Hungarian. His clothes, too, had the look of cheap copies of Italian sportswear.

"All right, buddy, show me your act," I said with (I hoped) sufficient bravado, although I was edging for the door just in case.

My strange visitor slung his case onto the battered school desk I used as a combination bar and typewriter stand. I flinched when he flicked the rusting latches up, but when he withdrew an interesting piece of carved and polished wood, I relaxed.

His instrument was of his own making. It was a queer amalgam of double bassoon and bass viol. He blew into the reed while bowing, and some of the frets had holes for fingering, so that he could bend notes with the strings and then change pitch when the holes were momentarily uncovered.

The music he made was like nothing I had ever heard, nor had the world. It wailed, it sighed, it crescendoed and diminuendoed with the fantastic overtones that his breath and that bow made.

Apparently the compositions he played were his own, though there were hints of Mahler and Sibelius in them. But more than the music was the emotional quality of the instrument itself, which seemed to cry and laugh and rage with the force of a living being. The effect was bewitching; I was entranced.

Here, in the space of ten minutes, I had seen two of the most fantastic acts I had ever, in all my years of show business exotica, had the pleasure and good fortune of witnessing. I began to think that maybe the golden-agers tour was a waste. We could go right to Broadway with this kind of talent.

"Thanks a lot—what did you say your name was?" I asked the musician/inventor with his unique string/woodwind instrument.

"I didn't say, but it is Simon Declaville. You can reach me at the International Hostel on Twenty-third Street."

"Yes, yes, we'll be in touch. Don't let anything happen to that instrument of yours."

"I sleep with it," Simon said.

I believed him.

"Well, good day," he said, uncertain if our short interview was over. I don't know why I had ever feared the man; he was obviously harmless. I had probably frightened him.

"I'll call you tomorrow. I'm sure we can do business, Mr. Declaville."

"Please hurry," he said over his shoulder as he went out the door. I thought that was an odd thing to say, but then you had to have that kind of odd mind to invent a string-bassoon, as he called it. I heard him humming distractedly as he descended the stairs. I was reminded of the story of Henry Cavendish, the man who discovered that water is composed of oxygen and hydrogen. He possessed such single-minded concentration that he locked himself in his laboratory for months at a time and had his food slipped under the door to him. To reach the elegant simplicity of mind necessary to understand water, he became a hermit.

Then there was the matter of the Hasid to consider. With two incredible new acts booked, if not actually signed, I decided to close up shop for the day and head over to Brooklyn Heights, where I might be able to get a lead on the man who wanted me for an observer.

At the foot of the stairs as you enter the subway is a newsstand—a battered tin shack no bigger than a closet, a cave within a cave, inhabited by Cincy O'Rourke, a seventy-year-old newsboy. Usually I could hear him hawking the world's miseries that passed for news, shouting the latest headline ("Russky consul takes a hit! Read all about it!") as I descended at Forty-fourth and Eighth. Today he was strangely quiet.

"What's the news, Cincy?" I asked and flipped him two quarters for the *Post*, as I always did.

"Don't ask," he said, and I saw that his eyes were reddened and moist.

"No, really, what's the matter, Cince?"

"My sister's granddaughter was on that plane."

"Oh, gee, I'm so sorry," I said, feeling helpless and foolish like I do when confronted with other people's losses.

"Only twelve years old, for crying out loud, and they're saying it was a bomb. What kind of maniac would kill hundreds of people, little girls? And for what? For some cause?" He wiped a shaky hand across his drained face and looked away.

I understood why he couldn't yell the news today. It was too close to home. It had become real. I wondered if the bombing was the work of a religious fanatic. Suddenly it seemed more important to find the Hasidic stranger.

3

Tikkun

The incident on the A train was mere coincidence, not part of my regular hobby of ferreting out these people; so I would have laughed off the event except for the Hasid's mysterious disappearing act.

I was a man on a magic carpet ride but I didn't know it. I was still trying to walk the streets and take subways like other human beings. This time the train trip to Brooklyn was a ride of terror. Wistful yearning was replaced by the surreal spirit-breaking violence of a bloody fight.

No one on the car interfered as two young blacks hurt each other with fists and knives. They fought silently, with the fierce brutality of prison inmates. Both were shirtless and both had the lean musculature and the crude tattoos of men from prison. Neither could defend himself so the struggle was a dazing series of unwarded blows and un-fended thrusts—they were killing each other.

Finally I couldn't take any more. I stood up slowly, but instead of intervening I took three small balls from my pocket and began to juggle while whistling "The Elephants' Parade." The two combatants, suddenly distracted, paused to look at me.

"Look at that fool," one snickered.

"Dumb honky!" the other spat.

The train pulled into the station and to my great relief a squad of policemen exploded through the parting doors (the trainman must have radioed ahead). The two bloodied youths bolted out the other door together, hooting at me and the clumsy, overweight cops who would never catch them.

I put the little balls away, my hands trembling like an old man's. The windows and doors and grimy floors of my end of the train were flecked with the sprayed blood of the fighters, a strange aerosol coating to the already painted scene. None of the police remained on the train, and it pulled out of the station a moment later on its way to Brooklyn. A panicked exodus from the car left me alone with the dripping aftermath. I staggered to a seat and eased myself down, feeling weary and wounded, as if I had participated in the bout. I held my head in my hands and, I have to admit, gave out a moan.

I was pretty sure I was alone. Well, I can't say for absolute sure; I mean, I didn't look *all* around before I sat down. But I know they lock the doors between cars these days, and we're yodeling downtown at forty-five miles an hour or so—so where did the rabbi come from, the one who was suddenly standing in front of me, the one who put his hand on my forehead to bless me and said, "Well done."

"Where did you come from?" I asked.

"Not one in a hundred would have done what you did. There is a great gulf between those who watch and those who act. It is called the abyss."

"It was no big thing," I said warily. I'm uncomfortable when I don't know all the facts, and this rabbi's unseen comings and goings unnerved me.

"Time," he said.

"What?"

"I used to have it in endless quantity. It was nothing for me to waste a day here, a day there. Now, when I need them, the days are so few. If only I had known sooner. Now I am unequal to the task. So sad."

"What task?" I asked. "Before, when we met before, you said you needed me."

"We need an observer."

"Yes." I waited, but tears were forming in the watery eyes of the old Hasid. He rocked back and forth rhythmically, chanting a prayer, the tears following age lines down his face into his patriarchal beard.

"It may be too late. And you, I must be sure. No, *we* must be sure."

"We? We who?" I pressed him, but then I saw the Brooklyn Heights station sign as the train creaked into my stop. I rose, towering awkwardly over the stooped rabbi. I put my hand on the sleeve of his black rabbinical vestment, but he shrugged it off, staring at the corner where the fight had taken place, as if he could still feel the lingering evil echoes of the recent conflict.

"Come on. This is my stop. I want to ask you more about this."

"No," he said. "Not yet. But soon. So little time is left me. A younger man such as you, a stronger man—" I had to yank my outstretched pleading hand back as the doors slammed shut, he still inside the train, me teetering on the platform between psychedelic delusion and pure crystalline reality.

The train moved off with my hand still groping for contact with the tangible, the actual, clutching at air like a supplicant from the madhouse.

Vowing to take cabs for a while, I trudged up the stairs toward Nathan Challah's bakery. Everybody calls him Nathan Challah, although his real name is Nathan Rosenblum. A survivor of the camps, he'd arrived in New York in 1947 and never left. In fact, he never left the magical ghetto of Brooklyn Heights, where Yiddish is still spoken and men like Nathan are prone to saying such things as "If you can—do!"

I used to visit Nathan when my spirits needed lifting, because I thought that if someone could survive what Nathan had survived, endure what he had endured, and still radiate joy, then there was hope in the world.

From half a block away came the scent of poppy-seed rolls in the baking. I felt better already. The old man had recently taken on two apprentices, who now did most of the work, allowing Nathan to do what he liked to do best —hold court at a table by the window of his small shop. Philosopher bakers are like philosopher barbers. They may know more than the Kants and Spinozas, the academicians and the intellectuals. Nathan enjoyed a constantly changing audience, his customers. His pronouncements consisted of a seemingly inexhaustible supply of Yiddish one-liners.

"'Villains fare well in this world; saints in the next world,'" he said when I had poured out my story—from the rabbi's first contact with me, the disturbingly synchronous news of the plane crash, the fight, and the rabbi's second visitation.

"The whole world is going to hell," I said.

"'Hell is not so bad as the getting there,'" the Yiddish philosopher quoted with a malicious twinkle in his eyes. I had to laugh. "It seems you have been chosen. Like my people. The chosen. But for what? 'The Bible contains more curses than blessings,' my friend. What do you suppose you were chosen for?"

"I thought you might be able to tell me," I responded, because I believed that Nathan Challah knew the rabbi.

"There is a Hebrew word for the task you have been appointed," Nathan said, and it seemed to me that he was dropping all pretense and telling me directly of his involvement, though he could have been talking in generalities. "It is *tikkun,* which means to heal, transform, and repair the world. That, and nothing less."

"Tikkun."

"Yes. Let me tell you a story."

4

The Golem's Young Wife

"Once," Nathan began, "there was a golem, a monster —one of the undead endowed with life by the forces of evil—a shapeless mass of a thing pretending to human form.

"This golem had taken the figure of a handsome young farmer. By day he scratched at the earth, but nothing will grow from the hand of a golem. Farm animals cringed at his touch, cows' milk soured, hens refused to lay eggs. So mostly this golem lay around in the daytime, preserving his malign strength for his nightly forays as himself, the evil one, the *schmurtz*."

"Was he Jewish?" I interrupted.

Nathan looked at me disgustedly. "He was a golem. He had no soul. How can a thing with no soul have any faith?" Without waiting for me to answer he continued: "By day he was a lazy farmer, but by night he was a child-killer, a slaughterer who thoroughly terrorized the entire region. Finally the men of the local villages mustered up the courage to meet in a barn and discuss the curse that plagued the neighborhood.

" 'We all know it's that lout from Plitensk who arrived here two years ago!' one shouted. 'I say we burn down his farmhouse, with him in it.'

" 'Wait just a minute!' the local rabbi interjected. "Undeniably, the horrors began when this Plitensk fellow arrived. But no one has ever been able to connect him to a single crime, other than sloth,'—for in fact it was our same lazy farmer whom they were discussing—'and we still must obey Jewish law, even in dealing with golems.'

"The talk went back and forth, with the rabbi playing devil's advocate more than he knew. In the end, the mob overruled the indecisive rabbi and marched to the golem's farm, torches in hand. But try as they might, they could not ignite the house or the barn or even the dry hay, for fire is one of the elements under the control of the dark forces.

" 'If we can't burn him, we should drown him,' the frustrated, infuriated crowd cried out, but drowning is a different matter. To drown a man, or a golem, you have to catch him. As darkness approached, the mob lost its enthusiam, and by twilight all had slunk away.

"The next day the villagers met again. During the night the golem had extracted a terrible toll from them—three more dead children were found. The neighbors argued bitterly among one another, yet nothing was resolved.

"Finally a young woman stepped forward and said; 'Let me see what I can do.'

"She was Bashele, youngest daughter of the village cooper. Bashele was the ugliest girl in the palatinate—stout-legged, big-nosed, coarse-haired. Aside from being ugly, she was completely unremarkable, completely ordinary.

She showed no special talent for anything, and except for being a devout daughter and competent housekeeper, she had very little to commend her. What could she do against the black heart of a golem?

"Nonetheless, no one else had any better suggestions, so Bashele set off on her own to the golem's farmhouse.

"The mob followed her; but when she arrived, they drew back. Boldly she strode up the rickety steps of the abandoned farmhouse the golem had taken up residence in. Throwing open the door, she strode in and slammed it behind her. The crowd held its collective breath, waiting for screams of murder, but nothing happened.

"That night, for the first time in months, there were no visitations by the golem.

"Within the week, Bashele had him repairing the front porch steps.

"After two months, he was attending temple services.

"By the end of his life, for he had begun to age almost as soon as he met Bashele, he was one of the respected elders of the area, and when he died, after a petition to temple leaders in Krakow, he was given a Jewish funeral and buried in holy ground.

"'What,' you may ask, 'did Bashele do to the golem?' And the answer is simple. She let the milk of human kindness flow. But that is not all. Yes, she gave him love, which kept him home at first, and she worked him so hard at the farm chores during the day that he was too tired to go out at night. But Bashele was wise in one more way. She taught him to love God, and so set his heart to yearning in that way which you too have felt, as you have told me.

"So," Nathan said, looking at me slyly, "do you know what the moral of the story is? How you and the *schmurtz* are alike?"

"Me and the *schmurtz*?"

"Yes. 'A person should live, even if only for curiosity's sake.'"

"It's hard sometimes," I said.

"'Nothing falls from heaven,'" Nathan admonished me with another zinger.

"What should I do now?" I asked.

"Obviously my story has made very little impression on you. Do you not see that your role is the same as Bashele's? You are to be somehow the bringer of *tikkun*. You must drop everything and obey the orders of this rabbi, who is certain to show up again."

"I don't know. I have a business to run."

Nathan shook his head slowly. "After all I have told you, that's all you can say? 'I have a business to run.' Take your bag of poppy-seed rolls and go." Nathan turned his back and refused to speak further to me. I left the shop dejectedly.

5

Indian Ruins

Suddenly my life seemed to be in disorder. A rabbi and an old Jewish baker seemed to be conspiring to draw me into some fantastic scheme with a premise I didn't yet accept, with a premise I didn't even know. I decided to do what any sane, red-blooded American would do: take a vacation.

With two incredible new acts booked, if not actually signed, I closed shop and rang up my travel agent.

"Why don't you wait a week and hop the cruise ship where your acts are going to play? You could take it as a write-off that way." Stanley was always looking out for my interests. He was also my accountant.

"I don't want to go to the Caribbean with a bunch of midget jugglers, Stan. And I don't want to leave the States. Things are too crazy right now."

"Huh?" he said. I realized that I was giving myself away. No one else was receiving visits from peripatetic rabbis.

"Look, just send me someplace interesting, out West. I don't care where."

"A surprise vacation! What a marketing concept! Okay, pick up your tickets after three."

"I'll send a messenger."

"Whatever."

I knew I could count on Stanley to ship me off somewhere interesting.

On the map the road was supposed to be paved. On the map it said Indian Ruins. But there were no Indian ruins, no kiva or ceremonial cave, no lodge, no pottery—nothing except a couple of drunk Navaho in jeans and T-shirts and scuffed cowboy boots and baseball caps. They were trying to decide if this crazed New Yorker was going to be able to get his Olds Delta 88 back down the muddy, rutted red-clay road to the highway without tearing off the muffler, or worse.

Cursing the rental car company that had substituted this behemoth for the subcompact I'd ordered, I pressed the button that rolled down the electric window and addressed the sorry pair.

"My map says there are supposed to be Indian ruins here," I said.

"Yer looking at 'em," one of the two replied, and they both cracked up. They tried to execute a pirouetting high-five, but, too drunk, they missed each other's hands and one fell over.

"Please, it's important."

"Up there," the one left standing gestured, pointing to a sheer cliff face of red sandstone, apparently accessible only by a narrow trail crisscrossed by deep arroyos, a trail that started right behind the pair, as I now saw. They'd been leaning on the tiny sign that pointed the way.

"Stop at the store on yer way out. Lots of stuff for sale there."

"Thanks, I will." I'd passed the store on the way in but hadn't given it a second thought. Now I decided I'd better go back there, since I wasn't about to do any hiking in the suit and loafers I was wearing.

In the store, the Southwest was being sold off, bit by bit. Obviously this was as close to the ruins as the two Indians thought I'd ever get. Sure, send the white man from New York to the tourist shop and we'll all be happy. Cardboard bins were strewn on the floor, each piled with rocks: fire agate, Apache tears, petrified wood, agate slabs, any sliver or hunk that might have some value. On the counter, varnished rattlesnakes vied for space with scorpions trapped in Lucite cubes.

Behind the displays stood an Indian woman, tall and ugly, with a face like a reptile's, wrinkled and dry, and hard lizard's eyes. She stared at me as if I were from another planet.

"He's waiting for you," she said.

That caught me off guard. I wasn't expecting it. I took it hard and could only reply; "Who?" which I knew she wouldn't answer.

She didn't. "Up there," she said, pointing silently through the neon Budweiser sign in the window to the red cliff face, bathed in a mystic late afternoon glow.

"Can you sell me some jeans and hiking boots?" I asked, trying to remain reasonable in the face of things. I didn't understand why everybody seemed to know why I was here.

"No," she said. "You better go now, before it's too late."

"Too late?" I asked weakly.

"It's a test, stupid."

I tore out of there and jumped in the 88. *Screw it*, I thought. *If the rental company wants me to use this monster, I'll use it!* and I slammed her into low and gunned the V-8. Halfway back to the trailhead, a big rut caught the front bumper and tore the license plate off, but I figured, *What the hell, you only need the rear one anyway for the cops*.

The two Indian clowns were gone when I parked at the trailhead. As I climbed up the path, though, I thought I saw them ahead on the trail, just rounding the next bend; and once I thought I glimpsed them huddled way above me in a tiny hollow on the cliff wall, but then I looked more closely and saw that it was only shadows.

The trail switched back and forth as it climbed. Soon I could look back at the landscape, a classic western valley, only the single road leading out of it around the far mesa, only the single building on that road, the combination store and gas station where I'd stopped.

Up ahead, when the trail met the face of the wall, there was an outcropping, a tall needle of sandstone carved away from the rest of the cliff. The trail snaked between it and the wall, and suddenly I was within a few hundred feet of the ridge to the next valley.

I looked ludicrous, of course. My suit was dusty, my shoes and pants were coated with red mud from wet places on the trail, and it was both silly and painful to be hiking in this outfit. The trail narrowed to a ledge, and I was now several hundred feet above the valley floor. But near the top there was a cavity, not a cave but more like a bowl with an overhanging roof. The trail gave out there. There seemed no way to surmount the overhanging projection short of using mountain-climbing techniques I wasn't about to attempt, either in or out of hiking gear.

I sat down in the depression, which had obviously been reached before, since there was a fire ring of stones set in a formal design and—I hadn't noticed before, there were faint petroglyphs on the rock ceiling. What an idiot I was. These were the Indian ruins!

Just as I approached the carvings, I heard a sound behind me and turned around. It was the Hasid from the A train.

"Shalom. Thank you for coming. I had to be sure you were willing. Sit down."

"You brought me all the way out here—ruined my suit —just to test me?" I protested.

He held up his hand to stop me. "Do you now agree to be an observer?"

"Yes, yes—" I said, not because I believed him all of a sudden, but it was a pretty good trick, his arranging to be here and hiring all those Indian actors—because that's what I thought they were. Under my breath, I cursed my ex-travel agent and accountant Stanley.

"Are you familiar with the legend of the Thirty-Six Just Men?"

"Uh . . . no."

"One of the tales of Jewish folklore, of which there are thousands, is the legend of the Thirty-Six Just Men, pillars of virtue whose saintly lives keep the world from degenerating into the chaos of evil."

"Their good vibrations, like," I said, but the rabbi ignored me and went on.

"Each generation is said to contain thirty-six such wondrous humans—common people, bakers, tailors, and so forth, unknown to one another. This legend happens to be true."

"And you're one of them," I guessed. The rabbi stared at me incredulously.

"Me, no, I'm just a poor sinner. The silent exertions of

the Thirty-Six keep the world in balance, negate the manifold evils of imperfect humans such as ourselves. But the balance is shifting. The power of the Thirty-Six is constant, or nearly so, but evil grows and grows. It has been decided that extraordinary measures are needed, a meeting, a meeting of the Thirty-Six."

"But they don't know one another. How can they meet? How do they get together?"

The rabbi shrugged. "It's a problem. Indeed, in the original legend it was suggested that a meeting would be disastrous. Yet, the state of the world is such that desperate measures must be considered. I've found three of them, but I need help. That's part of why you're here. They know they want to be found, but how to find them? Who better than a person of your interests to aid me in my search?"

"That's a bit more than being an observer," I managed to get out.

"Oh, you'll be that, too, once they convene."

"I'll help," I answered without saying I believed him. I wanted to believe. I wanted this to be the real thing, a conspiracy to save the world rather than destroy it. But it was too strange, him, up there, in his black coat, hat, and sidelocks; me in my disheveled, dusty, red-stained suit, high amid the mysterious remains of a former civilization. The thought crossed my mind that his coat was awfully clean considering the climb he must have just made, but then I remembered the petroglyphs.

Turning to look at them, I asked the rabbi, now that we were partners, "Any idea what these say?"

"Profound words of wisdom from the past. Our Native American forebears were succinct in their observations. This short epigram speaks volumes about the differences between two cultures:

White man build big fire, sit way back. Red man build small fire, sit up close.

Then I remembered thinking, *Funny, he hasn't told me his name*. I turned back to introduce myself, but of course he was gone.

6

Showtime on the Princess Maru

After my final encounter with the rabbi—somehow I knew I would never see him again (three visitations were the appropriate number and, in any case, he had laid out the scenario for me)—I knew what was expected of me. I cut short my Southwest vacation and flew back to New York.

Despite what anyone said to me, or how many elaborate magic tricks they played on me, I had a business to run. Before I could save the world, I had to make sure a pack of midgets and an eccentric inventor musician made the boat. Also, let's not forget the band, the tea dance instructor, the shuffleboard coach, the MC, and assorted other minor entertainers, according to the terms of my contract, I was responsible for providing to Maru Maru Lines.

Already this cruise was shaping up as a major headache. To be sure, I had uncovered fantastic new talents in The

Spuds and Mr. Declaville. But two acts do not a show make, especially on a week-long sail to the Caribbean and back for several hundred retirees. It took the rest of the week to audition enough material for a show. I had some banners and programs printed up: DEXTER SINISTER PRESENTS—BRING BACK VAUDEVILLE!

These old folks were going to see more spats and canes, hear more "Dutch" jokes, and smell more popcorn with real butter than they had in years. I didn't know how many of the dentured crowd were actually going to be able to eat the popcorn, but I wanted the zesty stale odor to pervade, as it did in the theaters of my dimly remembered youth— cathedrals of comedy, grand carpeted edifices of marble and granite such as the old Howard in Boston and the Palace in New York, where the popcorn aroma wafted up toward crystal chandeliers.

The Spuds strolled in to my office at eight in the morning on the day the ship was due to leave.

"What are you guys trying to do? I called every flophouse on the Bowery looking for you."

"You should have tried the Park Plaza," Fred, their diminutive leader, replied acerbically. "That's where we stay."

"Where's your luggage, your equipment?"

"We had it sent straight to the ship."

"Fine. So what are you doing here?" I was busy with a thousand last-minute details and didn't have time to babysit midgets. Even as I talked I had the phone pinned to one ear by a shoulder, as I tried frantically to come up with a replacement MC. My regular guy, a retired circus ringmaster, had backed out on me, claiming susceptibility to seasickness.

"We want to get a few things straight," Fred said, hopping up on my desk to put himself face to face with me. "First of all, we get top billing."

"No problem, Fred. You guys are the stars of the show. What I can't understand is why you're not stars already for some circus somewhere."

"Second, you booked us second-class cabins. We want staterooms."

Oh, Christ, I thought to myself. *Prima donna midgets.* "Fine," I said aloud, mentally subtracting the difference in room rates from my profits while I dialed another potential MC, hoping to find one who wasn't a dipsomaniac, a flake, dead, retired, or in prison. "What else?"

"Third, and finally, no pictures."

"Huh?"

"No picture taking from the audience, no publicity shots, no posing with the oldsters. Got it?"

"Sure. No big deal." This insistence on no photographs only heightened my suspicion that The Spuds were fugitive midget jugglers, maybe from another planet. Considering everything that had happened to me during the last week, it seemed reasonable. As long as they made their shows and didn't tear up the staterooms, I didn't care.

"All right, but no practicing in the rooms. There's a fully equipped gym on the ship and not too many of the geriatric cases are going to be using it. You can rehearse in there. Now get out of here and grab a cab to the *Princess Maru* at Pier Fifty-five," I said. "I'll be down there in an hour."

An hour. That's how long I had to find someone to host the show. Of course, I failed. Of course, I was going to have to do it myself. It seemed like I had to do everything myself these days. The world would have to wait. The Thirty-Six, if they really existed, would have to keep it together for another week, if they could. I was going to spend a week introducing surly jugglers to sleepy audiences and keeping the band from drinking too much before the last set.

7

The Rabbi's One-Twelfth

I thought I'd never see the rabbi again, but one thing stuck in my mind: He said he'd found some of the Thirty-Six. Three, if I remembered right. As I inched west across Forty-second in the back of a cab, heading toward the piers and an unwanted one-week time-out in my life, I kept thinking over and over, *What if there are Thirty-Six Just Men? What if there are?*

What did I believe? In the beginning was chaos. That much I knew. In my opinion, the cosmic blast that created the universe didn't do much except blow chaos across eternity. Now here was a clear set of events deliberately put in my path like a series of signposts.

Suddenly, although I was alone in the cab, I heard Nathan's voice in my ear, distinctly saying to me in his fractured Yiddish accent: "'All signs are misleading.'"

"What'd you say, buddy?" the cabbie wanted to know.

"Nothing. Hurry it up, will you. I've got a boat to catch."

"What do you want? You want me to drive on the sidewalk? You want me to call a helicopter? What?" The hack was right—traffic was backed up to the Hudson River. I could walk faster, but I had a big suitcase full of stuff.

"Forget it. Just keep going." *I should take my own advice,* I thought. *Just keep going.* I didn't ask for this assignment as some sort of Everyman representative to the Thirty-Six. I'd had it thrust upon me, as the saying goes.

The first day on the ship is always the most frenetic, with passengers settling in, and the crew shaking down the ship for the voyage. Although by the second day torpor sets in—after the continuous meals take their toll on the overstimulated digestive systems of the passengers, and everyone relaxes—it's that first night's show that sets the tone for the week: whether this will be a cruise where the passengers enjoy the entertainment or ridicule it. You have to get them into the swing of things.

Only one show was scheduled for the first evening, between dinner and the late-night buffet, not to be confused with the late-night room snack.

I wanted a whopper of a first show, but I wanted to save something for later in the week, too; so I asked The Spuds to hold back on their fancy midget-juggling and do some standard six-club passing for the first night. They grumbled a bit but acceded, seeing the logic of my request.

Mr. Declaville, too, agreed not to bring out his fantastic string-bassoon on opening night. I sought him out in his cabin after stowing my suitcase in my own stateroom. Mr. Declaville was in second class, two decks down, but his room was a pleasant one, small but neat, on the outside with a porthole.

Yes, he acquiesced, he would instead play a Bach sonata on an ordinary cello, if that was acceptable.

"Fine," I said. "The band is going to do some ragtime and some flapper tunes. You don't have to play with them. We'll give you a solo spot."

"I should hope so. Mr. Sinister—"

"Please, call me Dexter. My last name makes some people nervous."

"Mr. Dexter, perhaps I should tell you—" He paused, fumbling with some sheet music. His nervous fingers, so finely attuned to the stroking of horsehair against catgut strung over resonating wood, picked at torn corners of silent pages of notes.

"What is it, Declaville?"

"I'm not just a musician. That is . . ."

Oh, no, I groaned to myself, expecting another pitch for money. Now that we were on the boat and steaming down the coast toward the warm Bahamas, I was a virtual hostage to demands of the entertainers. "Look, Simon," I said, trying to be as charming as I knew how, "I know. You're an inventor. When we get back to dock I'd love to help you market your invention. I bet we could make a million. But right now all the remaining staterooms are booked, and—" Something in his look stopped me cold. Obviously I was off on the wrong track. "What then?" I asked.

"You're not going to like it. The rabbi sent me."

In the beginning was chaos. Now unseen forces were trying to impose order on my life. I rebelled. I grabbed Simon Declaville and shook him.

"What do you mean? Are you one of them?" I looked into his eyes, but I didn't find the saintly light I naively assumed would glow from the soul of a Thirty-Sixer.

"No. But the rabbi's one-twelfth are on this ship."

"Among the passengers?" I asked, terribly shaken, for there could be no doubt who he meant by the phrase. Only moments ago I had been thinking of them myself.

"Yes. Is it so surprising? The abode of a Thirty-Sixer is not, generally, the province of the young."

"What do you know about it?" I pressed him. "The rabbi was rather vague. You say they are older men. Isn't one born into it?"

"No." Declaville leaned toward me and whispered, I knew not why since we were alone in his cabin. "And you misinterpret me. I did not say—" He paused and changed his mind about whatever it was he was going to tell me. "But perhaps you would join us for dinner?"

Thus came my introduction to the true saints of the world, unseen heroes who have labored long and mightily to our benefit, who struggled now against the rising tide of evil. Who despaired that they may be losing, and who had sought me out.

8

The Classified Personals (Thank You, St. Jude)

I have always tried to keep my personal life and my business affairs separate. I have never dated actresses or acrobats. I have never socialized with show people at all, in fact. Now here were two radically different elements of my life colliding in the dining room of a cruise ship. If only I could have found a Master of Ceremonies to relieve me of this commitment. But what was I thinking of? Why belabor myself with recriminations? I was stuck.

My tuxedo fit poorly. My center of gravity appeared to have shifted downward a few inches in the years since I'd last worn tails. I looked like a buffoon, an aging bum crammed into society clothes for a benefit on his behalf. The top hat helped, but only a little.

Never have I felt less like assuming the role I was forced to play—charming bon vivant, mingler, party rouser. With a last disgusted look in the mirror, I perched the top hat on my head at a jaunty angle and set off for the combination ballroom and dining room where both dinner and the opening night show were to be held.

I entered the brightly lit hall, which glittered beneath gaudy fake crystal chandeliers and walls bedecked with a coat of fresh white paint set off by gleaming dark wood trim and polished brass fixtures. I eagerly scanned the dining tables, trying to sense which three of these assembled retirees were not ordinary humans but divinely inspired beings.

They all looked like escapees from a shoddily run nursing home. Canes abounded, along with a few metal walkers. Some of the women's hair was so blue it reminded me of Christmas-tree bulbs, glowing from within.

I spotted Mr. Declaville in the company of a pair of these sweet doyennes. Taking the last seat at a table for four, I introduced myself before he could perform his social duties.

"Ladies, my name is Dexter Sinister. Mr. Right Left, Host of Showtime! As the Master of Ceremonies for this evening's performance, let me welcome you aboard the *Princess Maru*."

"Thank you, young man. My name is Agatha Shaughnessy, and this is Lillian Rourke. We're retired seamstresses." That should have set off bells in my head, but it didn't.

"Delighted." I kissed both of their extended hands. Old folks go in for that sort of thing. Mr. Declaville coughed politely to get my attention.

"Excuse me, Mr. Dexter, but I think you're in the lady's seat."

"A thousand pardons." I leaped up to make room for a third retired spinster seamstress. Again large gongs should

have been ringing in my cerebrum, but they weren't, so
Mr. Declaville had to ring them for me.

"Mr. Dexter, may I present Velma Grace, our third and
last honored guest."

"You mean——" I wavered, not believing what I was
hearing. Simon Declaville nodded once. "But, but——
you're not even Jewish!" was all I could think to say to
them, as I gazed fiercely into their little-old-lady faces,
each as kindly as my grandmother's, but no more so. They
were so ordinary-looking, so unprepossessing, I was
mildly disappointed. Perhaps I let it show.

"You were expecting Mother Teresa, maybe?" Velma
ribbed me in a bad mock-Yiddish accent, thickened into
porridge by a residual brogue.

"Well, no, that is, perhaps. Well——" I was speechless.
The three giggled at me. I recovered slightly. "Velma, Lillian, and Agatha?"

"Yes." Velma answered me with a grandmotherly smile.

Was someone playing a monstrous joke on me? "You,"
and here I bent forward——and they too brought their heads
in close over the table conspiratorially,——"are among the
Thirty-Six I've been told about?"

They nodded together, and Agatha sighed the kind of
wise and sad sigh that only older people are capable of,
one that suggests the vast breadth of their experience and
knowledge in a monosyllable, or less.

"Name one human misfortune you've prevented in the
last six thousand years," I challenged.

"Because we've prevented them you haven't heard of
them, silly dear," Agatha chastised, as if expecting me to
be further along with the program.

"No. Right. All I can recall is war, famine, disease, plain
bad luck, and one disaster after another for millennia."

"It could have been worse." Agatha again. How could
you argue with that kind of logic?

"Show me what you do, how you do it."

"What, sonny?" Velma asked.

"How you work your effects on the unsuspecting world. How you do what you say you do, sustain the world with your goodness."

"I never stop. That's my secret," said Velma. "Agatha, how about you?"

"A miracle? You want a miracle?" Agatha asked me.

"Yes."

A button of my tuxedo popped off and came spinning down on the table. It whirled there for a long time. Too long. Agatha pinched it in midspin.

"I'll sew it for you, my dear. I always have needle and thread handy. It's an old seamstress's habit," Agatha said drolly.

"So do I," said Lillian, the quietest of the three.

"So do I," said Velma, the wisecracker.

"That's your miracle? Pretty small stuff, don't you think?" I was not impressed.

"Mr. Sinister, even if we have the whole world to save, we must sew the loose button on your suit."

"Why?"

"Because this is where we are now, and this is what we can do now."

"But, I was under the impression that your beneficence spread farther, much farther, was all-encompassing."

"It is. Or—it was, until the balance shifted. Now, we do what we can, a crisis defused here, a rescue operation there—would you like to know how we met, Mr. Sinister?"

"I'd love to, really, but I have to go be Master of Ceremonies in just a few minutes now, and I need to be backstage with the troupe. Can this wait until after the show?"

"Of course. You run along. We'll sit right here."

"Enjoy the show." Thoroughly unnerved, I fled backstage to the relative sanity of a room full of jugglers, tap dancers, and eccentric plate smashers.

I'd found a little girl the spitting image of Shirley Temple, who could sing "The Good Ship Lollipop" while tap-dancing on a rola-bola. She led things off, after a rousing introduction from me, and promptly proceeded to rola-bola right into the butter-cream cake on the dessert table. I guess balancing on a board atop a rolling cylinder is more difficult on a pitching ship than on land.

The little girl was led in tears from the stage, her frilly dress frosted with chocolate.

The band hemmed and hawed through a cheesy rendition of a couple of schmaltzy Al Jolson numbers, which stirred appreciative applause from the audience of septuagenerians and octogenerians, while the next act frantically prepared to take up the considerable slack left by my Shirley-alike.

At the appropriate moment, I signaled the band to conclude and strolled onstage from behind the flimsily rigged drape that hid the tiny backstage area.

"And now, ladies and gents," I began, trying to puff myself up like the vaude house MCs used to do, sounding like the glorified carny barkers they mostly were, all bluster and hyperbole, "you are about to witness the most extraordinary comic routine the stage has ever seen. A dazzling display of prodigious prestidigitation guaranteed to split your sides, curl your toes, and straighten your hair with laughter—the magic elixir that's good for whatever ails you. I give you Slam Bomsky, and his famous turn: 'In the Kitchen.'"

I have to confess this is my favorite act, and the band's, too. Whenever I can, I hire Slam, who was an authentic vaude star, and now, at the age of ninety, adds the comedy of the labored efforts of his shrunken, weakened body to his eight minutes of hilarity. Slam is an eccentric plate smasher. With a few dollars' worth of chipped china, he wows 'em.

Slam's act consists of building elaborate crescendos of plate smashing, sometimes a cappella, sometimes in rhythm with some nutsy tune from the band. Carrying out giant, swaying stacks of thrift-shop porcelain, he might drop one or two just reaching his place at center stage.

Setting the stack down, he might tilt it and one or two more place settings slide into ruin. But these are mere warmups for the series of drops, slips, bumps, and finally, all-out deliberate throwing and stomping of plates that follows.

There is something so primally satisfying about it that everyone gets into the spirit. On more than one occasion I've heard audiences urging Slam on, and once a woman rushed the stage to join in.

On this night, Slam finished up with a hundred or so saucers methodically hurled against a wall to the tune of Sousa's "Stars and Stripes Forever!" His bifocals dangled from one ear at the end, and he needed an assistant to help him off stage, to tumultuous applause.

The rest of the show went off without a hitch, and I was able to relax for the first time in a week. The closer was Declaville's sensitive playing of Bach's Third Cello Sonata, which would have been a crowd chaser in real vaudeville, but on this ship of sentimentality and remembrance was an unqualified hit.

I rejoined the three elderly Thirty-Sixers at their table.

"Wonderful show, young man. Mr. Declaville is certainly a master at his craft," Agatha complimented me and the string player at the same time.

"'You ain't heard nothin' yet,'" I crooned, copping Jolson's line that introduced sound to motion pictures and effectively killed vaudeville. Wait 'til these ladies heard the wonderful string-bassoon. Then I realized, they knew

Simon Declaville. They may even have provided him the
miraculous instrument, for all I knew.

"We were going to tell you how we met," Agatha began.

I had to keep reminding myself that these were members
of the legendary Thirty-Six, whom the rabbi had assured
me were real, and not the plain spinsters they appeared to
be.

"When I first understood the gravity of the situation,"
Agatha continued, "I knew that the ancient proscription
must be broken. There had to be a meeting of the Thirty-
Six. But how was this to be accomplished?"

"At last I settled on a method, which produced Lillian
and Velma here. I took an ad in the personals section of the
newspapers in several major cities. You've seen the type of
column I mean?"

I had seen pathetic printed "Thank You, St. Jude" messages for favors rendered, good health, whatever, that were
sometimes carelessly mingled with the relationship
ads—"Tall, shapely Princess looking for Prince Charming"—and the missed connection ads—"We met on the
Forty-second Crosstown, you were wearing a down vest
and liked Mozart." If this was the level of spiritual activity
practiced by the Thirty-Six, I was wasting my time on a
hoax. I told Agatha so.

"And yet, Mr. Sinister, it worked; for here are Lillian
and Velma."

"What do you expect me to do?"

Around us the waiters were clearing tables. We were the
last ones in the club.

"Let's take a late-night walk on deck," Agatha suggested. Surprised by this proposal from the frail-looking
woman, I nevertheless acquiesced. The waiters wanted us
out of there so they could close up.

The chill night air of the Atlantic had driven everyone
else indoors. The three ladies and I were alone as we shuf-

fled along the promenade deck. Lillian and Agatha used canes. Velma, though bent over with peritonitis, was able to do without one.

When we reached the bow, they stopped and unexpectedly circled me.

"What's going on?" I asked reasonably enough.

"It appears that you do not believe us," Agatha chided.

"Don't take it personally," I said. "I'm a skeptic by nature."

"Yes. Well, we've talked it over among ourselves, and we've decided that a demonstration is necessary."

"Oh," I said, waiting for another spinning button or some other simple magic trick.

"Yes," Agatha said again, and then she rose off the painted deck and into the sky, followed by the other ladies. Their brittle faded hair streamed behind them as they flew in formation over the cruise ship like albatrosses of fate, mocking my puny cynicism. Then they ascended and dematerialized into a dust of sparkles that quickly dissipated in the blustery Atlantic breeze. Head bowed, I walked alone until dawn.

9

Vegetarian Armadillos the Size of Armored Cars

I have always believed that the real world was magical enough without having to embroider on it. Once I heard a PBS nature-show host describe a time in the past when "vegetarian armadillos the size of armored cars" roamed the Brazilian *cervado*. Today's version is breadbox-sized and eats termites. The natural world is filled with wonders of equal or greater magnificence. So why do I need this? Why do I need here-again gone-again rabbis and grandmothers who fly and vanish into fairy dust?

Now, I had to admit, as I paced in the misty gray early morning light, they had made themselves plain to me. This was true magic, the magic of the immortals, which rests in truth and not deception. I had waited all my life for this moment. Why was I so anxious?

At dawn I crept into my stateroom and ordered a room-service breakfast. The thought of facing the mountains of food on the breakfast buffet was too much for me. I was a man dizzy from sights that should be hid from mortals.

In a way, I also dreaded seeing them again in their guise as little old ladies, which I am sure they would insist was all they were. Having viewed them silhouetted against the rear smokestack of the *Princess Maru*, I knew better.

After breakfast and a cramped but refreshing shower, I was able to think more clearly. I decided that in the interest of affairs, I should pay Agatha a visit in her cabin. I went straight to the ship's purser.

He told me that there were no such persons named Velma Grace, Lillian Rourke or Agatha Shaughnessy aboard the ship. By this time I shouldn't have been surprised at this turn of events, but I was startled and a little angry. I tramped down to second class for a word with Declaville.

As I approached his cabin, I heard the ethereal, deeply disturbing sound of the string-bassoon. A true musician, besides being a broker for the Thirty-Six, Declaville practiced many hours each day. The weeping, gasping instrument plied its emotional force even through the iron bulkheads of the *Princess Maru*.

At last he stopped and I was able to knock without interrupting him.

"Who is it?" he called out instead of opening the door.

"It's Dexter, Simon. I need to speak to you."

"Just a moment." I heard him close and latch the instrument case, then he let me in.

"What was that piece you were playing just now?" I asked, for it had moved me almost to tears.

"It's a modern piece called 'Last Flight of the Condor,' written last year, the year that marvelous bird became extinct."

"Written by whom?"

"Me."

"Remarkable. Speaking of flying, our three angels seem to have flown the coop. They're not on the passenger list."

"I could have told you that."

"Aren't they real? I mean, physically real? I thought each generation had Thirty-Six Just Men. Now there are women, and not Jewish, and they seem to be more spirit than flesh."

"Indeed. Perhaps that's what happens to true saints. Their bodies become so insignificant as to be dispensable. I'm sorry. That's the best answer I can give you."

"I want to see them again."

"Again, I'm sorry, but they decided you weren't the man for the job."

"What!" I was devastated.

"Apparently your cynical attitude drove them off."

"If I was cynical, it was because I, too, had to be sure of what I was getting into. Now I'm sure. And you're telling me that I've been rejected?"

Declaville said nothing. I staggered out of his cabin, my thoughts fixed on the struggle between the Thirty-Six and their foes.

Where do their enemies come from? How many of them are there? Already the dim suspicion was forming in my brain that if the Thirty-Six were humans, albeit highly developed, spiritual ones, then their foes must be humans, too. If that was so, they were badly outnumbered. And I, whom they had tried to enlist, had turned them away with my doubting mind.

10

1 Take up Diogenes's Lamp

For me, the rest of the trip was an agony of time passing in slow motion. I felt as though I was suspended in a giant vat of gelatin, motionless and globbed down, trapped on this voyage to nowhere. To make matters worse, we entered a fog bank soon after leaving port, and we spent almost the entire cruise under gray shrouds of mist that kept most of the elderly passengers indoors. Since the three flying spinstresses had disappeared, I could do nothing more in the way of starting a search for the Thirty-Six until I returned to New York. Meanwhile my responsibilities as cruise ship Master of Ceremonies pressed heavily on me.

Each night I had to stuff myself like so much human sausage meat into my tuxedo casing and pretend to be a jovial host with an endlessly entertaining stable of performers just waiting to dance and sing their hearts out for the crowd. What a joke. Besides the two seasoned acts, Declaville and The Spuds, and the very seasoned veteran Slam Bomsky, who was kind of a one-trick pony, if you get my meaning, I didn't have much going for me. Fortunately the band was decent, and the oldsters wanted to dance and carouse more than sit; so I was able to hold back the big stuff for the final night of the cruise, which was billed as The Grand Finale of Vaudeville!

Okay, so sometimes I'm a little hyperbolic. Comes with the territory. But this night The Spuds would perform their most awesome tricks and Mr. Declaville would let loose on the string-bassoon. It promised to be quite an evening. Cruise ship management had decked the place with red-white-and-blue bunting and crepe and passed out styrofoam straw hats to all the men and fake fancy hats to the women —some of whom wore their own real hatbox hats from the era, replete with feathers and spangles and jewels—so that if you glanced into the audience you might think you were looking at a real old-time vaude house.

The band warmed things up with a medley of Gershwin and Irving Berlin. Slam Bomsky reprised his plate-smashing sensation, this time taking on George M. Cohan's "Yankee Doodle Dandy" at a furious pace, strutting and dancing on nonagenarian legs, plates crashing in tempo to the driving patriotic march. I worried that Slam would work himself into such a frenzy he'd have a stroke right onstage, but old trouper that he was, he finished with a flourish, shattering some gravy boats, soup tureens, and enormous serving platters against a wall-sized portrait of Kaiser Wilhelm he'd unfurled.

The Spuds were terrific. How can you top midget jugglers tossing one another with no more concern for their bodies than if they were rubber balls? They added some Italian foot juggling to the fireman's-carry technique they'd displayed in my office and delighted the audience with a series of astonishing tumbles and somersaults performed as part of the juggling routine!

But the ultimate show stopper was Mr. Declaville's performance. Remember the scene at the end of the Marx Brothers' *Animal Crackers*? Harpo sprays everybody with sleeping gas and then sprays himself and joins them in a peaceful heap. Declaville's string-bassoon had the same effect on people. At first they were moved, some to audible sighs and moans, others to tears. Then a pervasive melancholy fell over the room, which after all was only a floating institutional dining hall draped in cheap decorations that suddenly had become a place enchanted. A sublime drowsiness crept into my eyes as the song continued. I noticed others fighting the urge to slip into a strange lull, not sleep but deep torpor, as if enveloped by the sound. We were like the characters in that wonderful old British mystery play, *Outward Bound*, passengers on an ocean liner who wake up to the gradual realization that they have left the real world and are wandering through hell.

I don't know how long I remained in that trancelike state after Declaville stopped playing—it may have been only a matter of a few seconds, but I couldn't swear to it. A steward who walked in at that instant told me later it was like being at Snow White's side when she woke to the prince's kiss, or sitting next to old Rip Van Winkle as he stretched. Mr. Declaville had left the stage, but there was no applause as the sleepy audience, realizing the show was over, slowly shook off the magical slumber and rose to leave. I knew they were more than satisfied.

Finally the agonizingly slow boat ride ended where it began. I rushed from the dock to my office and placed an ad in all three New York papers. In the classified personals, I pleaded with my missing mavens:

Velma, Lillian, Agatha. We met on a Caribbean
cruise. I was a doubting Thomas. You were into
flying. How about a second chance?   Dexter.

For three days I loitered in the office, hoping for a phone
call, pouncing on the mailman. No response.

I began to hang around senior citizens—in parks and at
cafeterias where they like to congregate—watching for my
absent trio. None whom I talked to could provide any information about them.

I called the City Directory, but they couldn't give me
anything either.

I visited the International Ladies Garment Workers
Union and went through the records of all the seamstresses
who had passed through all the union shops in the garment
industry. Nothing.

It was a muggy day in late July, the kind of day when the
pavement starts to look woozy and everything floats in a
stunned haze. I was wandering around aimlessly, sweating
in a pair of baggy jeans because my legs look like egret's
legs in shorts.

I found that I had strolled all the way through the garment district and down to Washington Square. The usual
crowd of street buskers, disco-dancing roller skaters, aging
bohemian chessplayers, artists, crack and marijuana
dealers, undercover cops, tourists, and NYU students mingled in the tiny park's eclectic bazaar.

Not in the mood for the noisy park scene, I skirted the
main walk through the arch and instead veered down one
edge. A plaque on one of the brick brownstones just off the
square caught my attention.

The marker signified the spot of the Triangle Shirtwaist
fire of 1911. "On this site, 146 workers lost their lives in
the Triangle Shirtwaist Company fire of March 25, 1911.
Out of their martyrdom came new concepts of social re-

sponsibility and labor legislation that has helped make American working conditions the finest in the world." I.L.G.W.U.

Now, what I did next you might think crazy, but you have to account for my state of mind when I did it. I was hot, tired, and depressed by my inability to locate three thirty-sixths of the world's virtue. Maybe it was the delirium of heat stroke, but somehow I got it in my mind that this would be a good place to try to invoke the missing three, this site of a great tragedy in the seamstress's profession. I wasn't even sure I knew what a Shirtwaist was, but I knew that many young women had died horribly here because of the greed and carelessness of owners who had ignored fire regulations.

I dropped to my knees and began to pray to them. "Velma, Lillian, Agatha. Come back. Please. I'll do anything you ask, just show yourselves to me once more." My pleas were not answered, except by the mocking stares of passersby.

Weary and emotionally drained, I sat at a bench in the park, trying to ignore the rumbling tribal beat of the conga team three benches down.

"Doesn't he look pitiful, dearies," I heard an elderly female voice say, obviously referring to me.

"Let's cheer him up, what do you say, girls?"

"Yes, let's."

I turned my head around, but if they were there, they were inhabiting another plane than the one I was on. I spoke to empty air.

"Agatha?"

"Yes, dear."

"Why don't you show yourself?"

"We're right here, dear, on the armrest." Three brilliant orange ladybugs fluttered on the curved grillwork of the iron bench frame. Christ, now I was talking to insects!

"Don't be alarmed, Mr. Sinister. Sometimes we travel this way, blown along by the wind. It's so much simpler than calling a cab, don't you agree?"

I could think of nothing to say.

"Now," Agatha continued, "I assume you're properly impressed with our credentials."

Again I thought silence was the better part of discretion.

"Good," she continued. "Your cold, cynical armor has been pierced, and we have found the warm heart beating beneath. Now, what we want you to do is help us find the rest of us. Newspaper ads are no longer sufficient. We need someone to do the legwork we can't handle anymore."

"Not even with six legs apiece?" I interjected.

"No. We need a detective, and you're it."

"Can't you even give me a clue as to where to start?" I pleaded, knowing the immensity of the task they were setting before me.

"Take up Diogenes's lamp, the light of the original cynic. Look for an honest man, for if a man is honest, then he knows the truth. If he knows the truth he has wisdom. If he has wisdom then he must have compassion, and compassion is the watchword of the Thirty-Six."

With these words in my ears, I watched the three lady-bugs fly away, and I could only hope they'd come again some other day.

11

Shopping for Bargains at the United Nations

This much I knew about the Thirty-Six: they were no longer confined to the Jews but apparently had spread by some means to represent the whole of humanity. On this Earth there is one place where nearly all the races and nations of the world are represented: the United Nations in New York, just a few blocks across town from my humble office.

I remembered the rabbi's warning, reinforced by my first meeting with members of this most secret of groups: the Thirty-Six are not known to the public. They are not the diplomats and politicians of the world but rather simple, quiet, dedicated souls who hide their value from the world and thereby preserve it. Still, it was worth a try.

Rather than take the tour, I called a minor diplomat I knew in the Indian consulate. I'd once smoothed out some trouble for him involving a touring Indian dance troupe that had landed in jail in the Deep South for promoting "belly-dance burlesque," as the charge stated. Their rendition of the Mahabharata was highly erotic, but I got them off on a cultural-exchange technicality. The Indian diplomat owed me one and was delighted to issue me a pass that gave me access to the main hall of the United Nations.

I wandered for hours through the halls: listening to the pastiche of languages, observing the colorful native dress of many nations—the wearing of which had recently come back into vogue after a long period where almost all the delegates dressed in Mao jackets or dull Western business suits.

Nowhere did I hear talk of the crisis feared by the Thirty-Six. I now understood their problem to be the general moral decay of the world, not attributable to any one event but rather the cumulation of many small sins built up until they were so monstrous they could no longer be concealed. As a global population, as a species, we were failing in the worst way: we were losing our moral imperative.

I eavesdropped in the cafeteria as eager young physicians prodded an African diplomat for more cooperation in supplying food and medicine to refugees from a neighboring civil war. Because the refugees happened to have encamped in an area controlled by revolutionaries against the government, the military leader of the country had cut off aid to them. Fleeing from one war, they had fallen into another. If the Thirty-Six were going to act, I thought, they had better hurry.

My day at the United Nations came to an end without my having discovered a single Thirty-Sixer. I trailed out of the massive monolithic building in low spirits. Gone was my innocent optimism. I had entered the Hall of Nations and left the Tower of Babel.

At the edge of the UN Plaza, just beyond blue NYPD

sawhorses put up to cordon off the area, was the usual collection of pickets, placards, and protestors, almost as diverse a group as that gathered inside.

Previously I might have passed them with scarcely a glance, but my antennae were up now. I walked the line of marchers, perusing each sign. One group sang Jewish folk songs, and my interest was quickened when I heard mention of the *Lamed-Vov*, the Yiddish name for the Thirty-Six Just Men. But their signs demanded that the Soviets let all Jews out of Russia.

Another group decried atrocities in Asia. A third declared that there were political prisoners in America. A fourth rebutted the claims of the third. Police were on hand nearby to prevent skirmishes between factions.

At one end of the straggling line of dissent, a solitary man stood silently, holding a neatly lettered sign that said simply: PREPARE

No exclamation point emphasized the word. No shouting, chanting, hand-clapping, shoving, or jeering accompanied the direct, straightforward message. The sign was small. The man looked more like a driver meeting a traveler he didn't know at an airport gate than like a protester.

I approached him cautiously. He was a small Asian man, middle-aged but prematurely wrinkled. He kept his eyes down when I first addressed him.

"Excuse me, do you speak English?"

"Yes."

"Okay, I'll bite, prepare for what?"

"Anything. Everything."

How to approach him? What do I say? I decided to go to the heart of the matter.

"Do you know the legend of the Thirty-Six Just Men?"

He raised his eyes to me, and I saw that he was one of them. Pure kindness flowed from his face, but it was mingled with a sadness so profound and encompassing that I stepped back and threw up my hands to shield myself from the face of compassionate love. In his mournful eyes I discovered the look I had sought in the three celestial women, whose plain and simple faces had fooled me, 'til they flew.

"You have found me, Buddha be praised."

"Come with me," I said and took his hand in mine, and felt the power there, though I still could not look him eye to eye.

12

Avatar of
the Can People

I was actually quite pleased with myself. I had just located the fourth of the Thirty-Six. I led Mr. Chin (for that was his name, I discovered, when I had calmed enough to converse with him) back to my office.

"Tell me about yourself," I said, after we had exchanged names.

Apparently he had been waiting and hoping that someone would ask him that question. With no further prompting he started in, speaking in clipped but precise English: "I was a boat person. One of many Chinese forced to leave Vietnam, which I called home. In 1979, my family and I attempted to cross the Malaccan Strait in an open rowboat with nineteen other people. My wife and two young sons drowned in the passage when our boat was swamped by a passing tanker. I clung to the overturned hull until I drifted to safety and was interned in a Philippine camp. Two years later I reached America.

"In Vietnam, I had completed my training to be a physician. In America, the only position I could attain was as hospital orderly. I lived in a rundown section of San Francisco—not a residential slum, but a neighborhood of abandoned warehouses and small businesses. My house was one of the few houses on the block, and through frugality and hard work, I had managed to save enough money to buy this house. My nearest neighbors were a burlap-bag warehouse, a chainsaw-repair shop, and an auto-refinishing plant.

"During the day there was much business, but at night my neighborhood was nearly deserted. This made it a convenient place for homeless people to camp in doorways, inside the burned-out skeleton of an old brewery across the way, and along the area beneath the freeway overpass, where they could find shelter from the rainstorms that swept through the city every winter.

"I did what I could to help others, especially my Vietnamese brothers and sisters. In the course of these efforts, I learned of the strange subculture of can collecting that had sprung up among my people: the can people.

"I went to see for myself. One of the big aluminum companies had set up a trailer truck to accept cans. A line of Vietnamese people stretched around the corner, interspersed with an occasional ordinary American bum—pardon the expression.

"Each person had a plastic trash bag or a supermarket shopping cart full of crushed beer and soda cans. The aluminum company was paying ten cents a pound for the cans, which came out to about fifty cans for ten cents, or a fifth of a cent a can.

"I saw one tiny old Hmong woman in a turban and embroidered vest and a dress so long it dragged on the parking-lot asphalt, with two bags, each quite a bit larger than herself, one on each end of a long pole balanced across her shoulders.

"A bag was emptied into a hopper, weighed, inspected, and then the can person was issued a scrip that could be redeemed for money or groceries in the supermarket. It was a convenient arrangement for the aluminum company, which didn't have to handle any money, and for the supermarket, which garnered the proceeds. Only for the can people was it inconvenient, ridiculously labor-intensive, and an absurdly low return on their investment of time and effort.

"I wrote letters to the city government, the newspapers, and the metal companies on behalf of the can people, and eventually the companies began to issue money instead of supermarket scrip and made one or two other changes in their procedures to benefit the can people. Suddenly I was taken for their leader."

I looked at Mr. Chin. He was slight, with the darkened skin of a farmer or someone constantly in the sun. It was hard to imagine him as a charismatic leader, until you looked into those eyes.

"The companies make it hard for the can people," he continued. "They make the can people bring the cans to them, instead of sending trucks around. They make the can people wait in lines to weigh it up; but they are only can people, who have no place to go, nothing important to do. That is what the bosses of the companies think.

"On a day off from my job as a hospital attendant, I hunted for cans myself. I was surprised to discover how many blocks I had to walk to find even one. In my journeys I saw and talked to many scavengers, often people like myself who had been respectable citizens in Vietnam but were lost here.

"I noticed that some of them had developed special

tools—long, hooked prods for scrounging in dumpsters or fishing cans out of sewers. Others had strung burlap sacks around their waists or over their shoulders to avoid carrying the awkward and undependable garbage-can-liner bags.

"At the end of a tedious day, I had about sixty cans— twelve cents' worth. Still, it was enough to give me an excuse to visit the recycling center.

"When I reached the back of the parking lot, I found that the trailer truck was gone. A notice taped to the wall notified all persons interested in recycling cans that the trailer was now parked across town behind another giant retail food-chain store.

"I would have liked to have taken a bus, but the bus drivers had recently threatened to strike if the can people were allowed to bring their leaking, in-danger-of-bursting bags aboard. A city ordinance had been rushed through to prevent this inconvenience. So I walked the several miles to the new locale. A crowd of cannites, as I thought to call them, waited at the trailer door, which was shut.

"I listened to them for a few minutes as they spoke of the injustice they endured. As I talked I saw that they looked upon me as their leader, that they hoped I could lead them to some new future. They came up to me, complaining about the hardships of their lives, and suddenly I realized that my duty extended far beyond this ugly, sterile parking lot—to the whole world.

"As I felt their unspoken yearning, in a moment of revelation, I knew myself to be one of the Thirty-Six. I don't know if this is how it happens for each one of us, but that is how it happened for me.

"We cannites began to organize. Instead of working alone, we pooled our resources. We divided up territories, so that no one was searching already cleaned bins and dumpsters. New tools were developed, and successful designs passed along. Those few among us with automobiles ran pick-up routes, collecting the day's haul to bring to harvest at the recycler.

"We opened our own soup kitchen, specializing in Chinese and Vietnamese food. Oh, in so many ways we improved our lives. A succession of small miracles, you might call it. The children we placed in schools, even if their parents still lived in abandoned automobiles under the freeway. We moved as many families as we could into permanent housing. We were able to find jobs for some of them. The immigrant community was strengthened and nourished. And with each act I felt my powers grow, and the communion between myself and invisible helpers increased."

"Invisible—oh, you mean the others of the Thirty-Six?"

"Yes—I felt them, knew they existed, but never contacted them, nor had the urge to, until recent events demanded it."

"You felt compelled to extend your circle of good, is that it?"

"I couldn't remain and be a leader to the cannites. I quit my job and fled here to New York. I tried to attract the attention of the others, for I sensed that the time had come for us to meet. You are the first one I've managed to reach—"

"Oh, no," I said quickly, stifling a laugh, "I'm just a hired hand, Mr. Chin. But I know some ladybugs who are anxious to meet you."

"I beg your pardon?" Mr. Chin said, understandably confused.

"Never mind, Mr. Chin. Welcome to Dexter Sinister's Variety Arts Talent Agency."

"Thank you. But about the others—"

"We'll have to work together to find them." I still had a question or two for Mr. Chin. "So, that's it?" I asked.

"One day you were a hospital orderly, the next you were a Thirty-Sixer. No special training?"

"None."

"No signs or anything? You just felt the call, and that was it?"

"Well, there was one manifestation, if that is what you mean."

"Manifestation?" I asked warily.

"Of our power. Isn't that what you were asking about?"

I nodded uneasily, not wanting to provoke him, remembering the last time I let my unfortunate cynicism show.

"Yes," Mr. Chin confirmed, "the day I realized my true calling in life, an extraordinary thing happened. It reminded me of the Chinese fairy tale of the fisherman's wife who wants more and more. I wanted to do something for the can people before I left."

"Yes?"

"I felt their unspoken wish and willed it to be—a small mountain of aluminum cans appeared in the parking lot. The can people rejoiced and began stuffing the cans into bags. The aluminum company had to bring in eleven extra trailer trucks."

13

My Yiddisher Mafia

The hunt was on in earnest now. Velma, Lillian, and Agatha showed up at my office, unbidden—in their human form, thank God. They and Mr. Chin embraced in an emotional moment I could share only vicariously. It was soon agreed that the three ladies would staff the phones in my office while Mr. Chin and I were in the field. This gave us a command post for the operation. My success in finding Mr. Chin at the United Nations gave me another idea for the search.

"The people we seek know who they are, and they want to be found," Mr. Chin said. "But if you have any doubts, bring the person to us. We will know."

Mr. Chin's comment set me to thinking of a Tolstoy short story, "God Sees the Truth but Waits," one of the simple moral fables he wrote near the end of his life when he had become a devout Christian and a vegetarian. The story's moral is evident by its title. Justice is inevitable. Life is fair. In the end, no one escapes the reckoning. As city noises rumbled in through an open window, I let my gaze wander over the three elderly women and the middle-aged Asian man who comprised the tiny portion of the Thirty-Six I had stumbled on thus far. Here were my representatives of "God's honest truth," as my grandfather used to say.

We alone on the planet were aware of the coming catastrophes that would plague the world if the Thirty-Six couldn't stem the moral ebb tide. At least, the Thirty-Six knew. I took it on faith. Suddenly I had an inspiration.

"Mr. Chin, please drink your tea. I just realized I already know where to look for our next companion."

Back to Brooklyn I went, Mr. Chin in tow like a dinghy pounding through the waves behind an ungainly sailboat. Nathan was deeply involved in the events that had led me to the Thirty-Six. He might be one himself, for all I knew; but even if he wasn't, he was my guide into the underworld of Brooklyn Heights and the Jewish community there. I was sure I would find a representative or two of the Thirty-Six among these people, from whom the legend of the *Lamed-Vov* had originated.

We took a cab across the Brooklyn Bridge into the Heights.

Nathan sat at his table as usual. He barely acknowledged my presence when we entered, but as soon as he caught sight of Mr. Chin, his manner changed instantly.

"Oh, revered one, I am honored."

I honestly believe he would have dropped to his knees if Mr. Chin hadn't laid a gentle hand on his shoulder.

"How did you know?" I asked Nathan, who had ignored me until that moment. "I mean, you could hardly mistake him for Moses, now, could you?"

"The light from within shines through," Nathan answered, still diffident and humble in the presence of this spiritual giant.

"Thank you, my friend," said Mr. Chin. "Although eating bread is not native to my culture, your bakery smells so wonderfully. May we break bread together, as is your custom?"

"Of course, of course." Nathan jumped up and hurried behind the counter to bring out his freshest steaming bialys.

I told Nathan of my progress in locating the Thirty-Six. All the while he stared at the *Lamed-Vov-nik* before him with the greatest respect and reverence.

"Why have you come back to me?" he asked.

"There must be members of your community who belong with Mr. Chin and my three lovelies."

"Not according to Andre Schwartz-Bart. In his novel, *The Last of the Just*, the last of the Levys chosen to be one of the *Lamed-Vov* died in the concentration camp."

"Is this what you believe?" I asked.

"I don't know. Today's transplanted Jew is so materially oriented, so worldly, so un-Orthodox. I don't know if there can be any holy men here."

"Oh, but there must be," Mr. Chin stated calmly. "Our whole scheme of things depends on it. Help us find them, to ensure that the coming judgment is universal."

This was the first I'd heard of a judgment. Up until now I'd understood the role of the Thirty-Six as being that of savior, preserver of the balance of good against evil. I looked at Mr. Chin curiously, but just then Nathan Challah spoke up: "'If a judge won't make a decision, the Code of Laws can go to hell,'" he intoned. "I'll help."

In recruiting Nathan, of course, we got not only him, but his whole network of kibbitzers, schmoozers, and shake-a-legs. They spread out through the borough, passing the word that the *Lamed-Vov* were resurrected, and that anyone knowing of a likely candidate should contact them.

Soon a steady stream of would-be Thirty-Sixers—mostly rabbis but a few bakers, tailors, and shoemakers—were appearing at the offices of the Variety Arts Talent Agency. This was better than auditioning vaude acts, let me tell you. Apparently there were a lot of pretenders to virtue. Some faltered over visions of money and power. Others were too sensual, or too enamored of their own goodness. Each seemed to have some fatal flaw that prevented him or her from attaining true grace. Never once did the four true representatives consult about a candidate.

"When he or she walks through that door, we will know," Mr. Chin said, echoing his earlier words on the subject.

I began to grow doubtful of this line of strategy and was about to abandon it when Nathan telephoned me.

"I've found him!" he shouted triumphantly. "He's on his way. Our contribution. Thank you, Dexter, for the opportunity to meet these saints. This old man rejoices, that his eyes have seen such sights."

The five of us anxiously awaited the arrival of the latest prospect, for that's all I could consider him until he received the seal of approval from the four.

It was after sundown on Friday when we heard the grating sound of the front door to the street being opened. Vandals had long since broken the lock, so no one had to buzz to get in anymore.

Whoever it was climbed the stairs almost silently, feet barely sounding against the worn wood. With suppressed excitement we awaited the knock on the rippled glass of my office door. At last it came, a timid, hesitant tap.

Because it was my office, I took the initiative and opened the door.

And a child shall lead them, I thought, as a young boy

entered the shabby offices of the Variety Arts Talent Agency. His innocent face glowed with optimism. Instead of being garbed in the formal white shirt and wool slacks of a Yeshiva student, he was dressed like a typical kid from Brooklyn, in a T-shirt, jeans, and sneakers. Instead of wearing his hair long with sidelocks, he had it closely cropped. On his shirt was silkscreened:

FACTS ARE NOT THE TRUTH.
Ambrose Bierce

Only his yarmulke, a paisley job that barely satisfied rabbinical requirements, identified him as a Jew. Just to break the ice I pointed to his epigrammatic T-shirt.

"What does that mean?"

"It means, judge with your heart, not your mind."

The other four people in the room were acting strangely. Already I sensed that I was in the presence of a special individual. But I thought it was just me. Only when I saw the other four Thirty-Sixers paying homage to the boy with bows did I fully comprehend the dazzling radiance of his aura.

"What is your name, my son?" Mr. Chin questioned him gently.

The boy shifted from one foot to another and scratched his head. "Joshua Levy."

"How old are you?"

"Just turned thirteen. My bar mitzvah was last month."

"Do you know why you are here?"

"I . . . I think so."

"Tell us."

"The world is sinking."

"Where is it sinking?"

As Mr. Chin questioned Joshua, I was reminded of the dialogues of the Zen masters, those peculiar conversations called "dharmic combat" that monks engaged in to sharpen their understanding. To outsiders this verbal sparring often sounded like gibberish. To the monks, it represented a dialogue of the secrets of heaven and earth.

"Sinking into the pit."

"Yes. And what do you do about it?"

"I pray."

"When you pray, what do you pray for?"

"I pray for goodness to return."

"Where has it gone?"

"I don't know where it's gone to, but it's gone from the hearts of my people."

"Welcome, my son." With those words Mr. Chin hugged the boy. Velma, Lillian, and Agatha surrounded him like lionesses around a pride's favorite cub. I hung back, amazed at the sight of these extraordinary, supernatural beings fawning over a punkish pubescent teenage boy with a rebelliously patterned yarmulke.

"So," I asked Mr. Chin, just to make sure, "Joshua here is one of you?"

"The only true descendent of the original Thirty-Six. We have found him."

I studied Joshua. He glanced at me briefly, and I thought I saw a fleeting sign of a smile on his serious young face.

"Don't worry, Mr. Sinister," he told me. "Soon we will be united, which is more than Evil—which works selfishly only for itself—can do."

And a child shall lead them. And a talent agent shall gather them up. And they shall meet to save the world from itself.

14

Dexter Sinister, Cosmic Detective

Joshua Levy continued to exert a powerful sway over the other four of my little clan. I couldn't help but think of a young anointed questioning the elders of the temple, except that here they were all of the same persuasion.

Although there were no villains among us, just outside the offices of the talent agency was the grim panorama of Times Square. I decided it was better for me to work by myself, since I couldn't risk losing any of the Thirty-Sixers I'd already collected.

Monday found me on the streets again, sleuthing alone for innocent men. Do you know how difficult that is? Guilty men leave behind endless perceptible clues—ripped-open safes, dead bodies, getaway cars. Innocent men leave a trackless trail of small, invisible good deeds.

How do you look for the anonymous? Over and over my

search came back to this conundrum. The next Thirty-Sixer might be a postman in Poughkeepsie—or a fruit picker in Fresno, a continent away laboring in some corner of an immense orchard. How could I possibly get a message to all of them?

I needed a gimmick, some showy way of attracting attention to our cause without alerting anyone who might oppose us. I thought I might be able to plant a news-wire story without giving too much away, if I could come up with a media-catching event. I walked across town to the Four Roses Bar down the block from the Times Building. Usually I could find my buddy Dick Smith there after the evening rag was put to bed, and he was the guy who could help me with this; but I couldn't let him know what was going on, because he had the black cynical heart of a newspaperman. He'd laugh in my face if I told him what I was really doing.

Sure enough, he was stashed in a back booth at the Four Roses. The bar was a cool, dark, cavernous place, a workingman's bar that still served a free lunch of pickled herring, tomatoes, pickles, mustard, and onions. A real anachronism it was.

"Dick, what's news?"

"Well, if it ain't Dexter Sinister, our cosmic detective. Showed up any fakers lately, Dexy?" Dick knew of my propensity for unmasking the charades of spiritualism. He did not know that I'd finally stumbled on the genuine article.

"Can't say as I have, Dick. J&B on the rocks, Phil," I informed the bartender. I'm no saint, even if my office is full of 'em.

"So tell me, what weird acts are you touting these days?"

"Oh, I've got some midget jugglers and this musical novelty act that's pretty amazing," I said without much enthusiasm. "But listen, Dick, that's not why I dropped in." Phil slid a tumbler in front of me and slipped a napkin under it. "I want to get something out over the wires."

"What?"

"I've got an idea for a promotion for one of my acts—I need to get the word out big, national, international if possible," I improvised, making it up as I went along.

"What kind of act?" Dick Smith wanted to know.

"Ah, it's a magic act. And, uh, I need to find real simpletons, you know, innocent people, to be subjects for the show. I was thinking along the lines of 'Vaudeville Needs a Few Honest Men', something like that."

"What's this all about?" Dick inquired, his newshound's nose sensing a story.

"Just vaude hype, Dick, that's all."

"What does this magician do?"

"Uh, it's not one guy, it's a group. They read minds, but only those of pure simple folk, you know, small-town America."

"Sounds like you're getting your hobby and your profession mixed up," Dick commented, not knowing how right he was.

"So, what do you think, will the wires go for it?"

"Nah. You need something catchier. Justice and goodness are boring, Dex. You oughta know that. You got to show a little leg, something sexy, you know, before the wires pay attention. How about a Miss Justice pageant where all the girls have to wear togas and carry scales?"

"That won't do, but you just gave me an idea," I said. "What about a contest to find the nicest people in America, or the world? We could get people to make the nominations and I'll do the judging, and we won't tell the nominees" (*or you*, I thought to myself) "the real purpose of the contest 'til they win."

"Sort of like the Bus Driver of the Month campaign,

only for Good Men, huh? That might go over. How about the Good Guy Awards?"

"Or Good Folks. That might do."

"The Good Folks Award. I'll see what I can do."

Within the week my campaign was in full swing. From all corners of America came letters of endorsement for good people. I had succeeded beyond my expectations and also far beyond the capacity of our little group to respond. Mailbags full of recommendations poured into my office. The three ladies, Mr. Chin, and I struggled heroically to put some order into the stacks of suggestions.

Joshua read the best of the letters we gleaned for him: "'So-and-so contributes regularly to the Church Relief Fund.' 'So-and-so is a civic leader.' 'So-and-so likes children and dogs.' Don't people understand how much more is required than this? Perhaps your advertisement is misleading, Mr. Sinister."

"It's the best I could come up with at the time, Joshua." I felt his disappointment. I didn't want to let him down, this holy youngster who looked at me with sad eyes always more poignant in a child's face.

"Surely among these thousands are some of the ones we seek, if only we can identify them," Mr. Chin said hopefully.

At last one letter from a housewife in Maine seemed to touch on the qualities we sought. It read:

You ought to meet Mr. Andrew Scoggins. No one knows him outside of our neighborhood, but around here we all respect and admire him. He has been a farmer for over sixty years, raising only vegetables, because he doesn't believe in slaughtering farm animals. Now that's not that unusual, because we've got a lot of Seventh Day Adventists in the county, but Mr. Scoggins doesn't seem to have any religious persuasion of that kind. He always just seems to do the right thing.

The letter went on to describe the many times Mr. Scoggins had settled local disputes with wise counsel, helped struggling farmers with favors of money, time, and hard work. We conferred briefly and determined that a trip to Maine might be profitable.

My grandmotherly aeronauts offered to transport me, but I opted for a commercial flight.

15

Potato Power

Despite the beneficence of the Thirty-Six, maintained by my five as they sorted mail and stuffed envelopes at the office and by the other Thirty-Sixers wherever they might be on this globe—despite this continuous outpouring of unremitting love, mankind lumbered toward its own destruction like a maddened beast.

Little things tipped the scale away from civilization toward the barely suppressed savage urges of its heritage. There was an outburst of random shootings between irate motorists on the freeways of Southern California, an occurrence previously confined to wilder regions such as Mexico City.

Riots at soccer games grew more violent, with whole stadiums going up in flame and a horrifying loss of life. More planes dropped out of the sky, more ships foundered and sank, more trains derailed. The capillary-thin skin of organized society was peeling away, and exposed nerves twitched with spastic and dangerous reactions.

Amid the growing general calamity, I flew to Bangor and took a puddle-jumper farther north to Ashland, the heart of potato country. I rented a car and drove out into the endless fields, flat and seemingly lifeless, for the potato gives little evidence of its subterranean growth activity.

Mr. Scoggins's farmhouse was a simple white clapboard structure with red trim. Several whitewashed outbuildings crowded close by, as if huddled for company in the open barren expanse.

Mr. Scoggins greeted me at the door. I realized at that moment that without one of the five with me to validate him, I could only make my best judgment; but I still felt it was safer than bringing one of them out into the failing, perilous world.

"Mr. Scoggins?" I asked.

He nodded affirmatively.

"How do you do?"

"What can I do for you, young man?"

"Didn't your neighbor tell you? You've been nominated for a Good Folks Award."

"What sort of nonsense is this?" Mr. Scoggins retorted, his Down-Easter accent like the bite of a tart Maine apple, as *sort* came out sounding like *saht*.

Not yet willing to abandon my cover, I faltered on. "My agency is looking for good people to represent their product," I lied. "Can we sit on the porch here while you tell me a little bit about yourself?"

"No, sir," he said, his eyes crackling with suppressed humor, "but I'm goin' out heah to slop the hogs, an' you can accompany me if you can stand the smell."

"Delighted," I replied, though once again I was inappropriately dressed for the occasion in suit and dress shoes.

"The porkers don't care if you're all duded up," Mr. Scoggins observed. We shuffled around the back of the farmhouse where a low barn housed a dozen or so sniffling, shoving hogs. Mr. Scoggins dumped some cracked corn and millet in the feeding trough.

"I understand from the letter we received about you that you're a vegetarian. Why are you raising hogs?"

"Because I like 'em," Mr. Scoggins replied, his flinty voice betraying a cackle of pleasure at this city slicker's confusion. But everything he said to me was forthright and pointed.

"You raise hogs for fun and potatoes for profit, then?"

"Nope. I like potatoes, too. There's a lot you can learn from a potato."

"Oh? Like what?"

"Did you evah see a potato clock?" Mr. Scoggins asked.

I confessed that I had—assuming he was referring to the child's toy where you plugged the prongs of a special clock into a potato and it ran for days on the electrolytes stored in the watery flesh of the potato.

"That's the item." Mr. Scoggins beamed, pleased that I knew what he referred to. "Think about it. All that energy, stored in a potato."

"So?" I said, underwhelmed. If I wanted this kind of stuff I could read the *Farmer's Almanac*.

"The potato is humble. It lays low to the ground. That's a quality more people could cultivate," Mr. Scoggins rejoined. "I nevah yet met a potato I didn't like."

I still wasn't sure about this cagey oldster. Would the direct approach work with him as it had with Mr. Chin? I probed a little more.

"Now, Mr. Scoggins, I told you before that you were recommended to us, and I told you that we were looking for you. Let me ask you something. Were you looking to be found?"

Scoggins scratched at his stubbly beard, an old man's beard, more like a tough perpetual three-day growth that razors can't conquer. "Now that depends. I refer you to the potato again. Does a potato hide in the ground because it wants to be found? If I wanted to be found for something, is this a good place to be?" He gestured to the vast emptiness stretching away in all directions from the cluster of buildings where we stood.

"You didn't answer my question, Mr. Scoggins."

"I didn't, at that. Been a time since I wanted or needed anything, but the news is mighty bad out there, ain't it?"

"Yes, it is," I said cautiously with a growing realization stirring in my breast.

"Lot of sadness, lot of human misery. Seems like I can't do enough for folks anymore. I fix their tractor, and their milker breaks down. I mend their horse's foreleg, and it falls in a ditch and breaks its neck. Don't know what the world's a-comin' to these days."

"And so, you've been hoping someone would find you, haven't you?"

"Yes, but you ain't him. Sorry, but you ain't the one I'm waitin' for."

I was stung by the remark, but Mr. Scoggins was matter-of-fact and didn't mean it as an insult. Clearly I had no special aura like the beatific representatives I had encountered, including himself. "No, but five of them are sitting in my office right now, hoping that my mission is successful. You're a Thirty-Sixer, aren't you, Mr. Scoggins?"

"I guess you found me out. How about a bowl of fresh mashed potatoes before we go?"

16

The Shofar Sounds

The morning after my return from Maine with Mr. Scoggins, Simon Declaville appeared. Instead of the familiar string-bassoon, he carried with him an instrument case that resembled that of a French horn, perhaps, or even an English horn.

He stood in the doorway, humming nervously as before. I hadn't quite forgiven him for the way he misled me about his deep involvement in this business, but he was clearly a big favorite among the Thirty-Six. They tugged him into the room and surrounded him, greeting him with hugs and handshakes.

"I have a place for all of you," he said.

"Wonderful!" I shouted, because frankly I was eager to get my office back and have a little time for myself. But the Thirty-Six, or at least the six (one-sixth now) gathered there were not as interested in the news as in admiring Mr. Declaville, and most especially his instrument case. With loving care it was placed on a cleared spot on my desk. Then I noticed a bizarre ritual occurring: each of the Thirty-Six silently implored Mr. Declaville by gestures and signs to remove the instrument from its vinyl fake-leather binding and play. He politely demurred, indicating in pantomime that the time had not come.

He led us, the whole troupe, out of the grimy building and onto the funky crime-infested streets of Times Square. We walked past Nathan's Famous and headed uptown on Broadway, through Columbus Circle.

Young Joshua helped his elders across crosswalks and assisted them in their halting and painfully slow passage. I wondered why they didn't fly, but who was I to interfere, for suddenly I felt like a tag-along among these giants of spirit. Perhaps this was their final walk through the fallen world.

At Sheep Meadow, next to the Strawberry Fields memorial for John Lennon, someone had erected a large Bedouin tent. This peaked apparition, apparently, was our destination.

Simon proudly led the group into the center of a flimsily roped-off area around the cotton structure. This hemp line, though frail and unimpressive, nonetheless had seemed to keep out all intruders in his absence.

Immediately the six repeated their supplications. Simon Declaville repeated his silent refusal. At last, after many requests, he acquiesced, though he made it clear without speaking that the number he was about to perform was merely a prelude to the song he still refused to play.

With infinite care he laid the black leatherette case on the ground in front of him. None of the members had as yet entered the tent. All stood outside the tent flap to the only opening in the canopy, which glowed from within even in the late afternoon sunlight.

Snapping open the brass clasps, Declaville withdrew a magnificent ram's horn, untouched by the hands of human craftsman. It was unaltered, natural perfection.

Placing his mouth to it, Simon blew a long single lingering note, mournful and plaintive, as sad a sound as I had ever heard. Immediately people began pouring out of their apartments on Central Park West, and from as far east as Fifth Avenue, south from Fifty-ninth Street, and even north from 110th Street and Harlem—people of all ages, backgrounds, and persuasions ran from their ordinary pursuits toward the source of the sound.

In a single magnificent wail our cover was blown, my little shepherded flock was sent out into the world, the careful conspiracy I had built exposed for all to see.

Within an hour, a million humans ringed Sheep Meadow. The cord kept them back, how I do not know, from the meager space of grass surrounding the tent where the six had withdrawn. I would no longer need newspaper advertisements or clever promotions. Simon Declaville had proclaimed the coming New Age with a one-note solo.

17

New Jerusalem
on the Green

The story of the holy campers in Central Park soon spread worldwide. At first, the NYPD had a difficult time controlling the crowd—there were the usual pickpocketings, shoving matches, and drunken brawls associated with such events. Then Mr. Declaville took to blowing that lone blues note on the quarter-hour, like some demented version of a Westminster chime. Each time he sounded, the enormous gathering quieted instantly.

The tent glowed periodically, modulating and pulsating as if some tremendous energy were growing within. As each new Thirty-Sixer passed through the otherwise impenetrable circle, the crowd would sigh in unison. Extraordinary humans had come to us from everywhere. The media had recorded the sound and broadcast it around the world. We were joined by a tailor from Tashkent, a baker from

Budapest, a noodle-maker from Nagasaki. It was miraculous.

And Joshua gave sermons. He retold parables from the Bible, and sometimes he made up his own. He stood in front of the impenetrable tent, calm in the face of the highly charged crowd, the police, the crush of media with their intrusive cameras and microphones, and he preached in the allegorical style of his predecessor.

"Listen to this story from the Talmud, called: 'The Spirit of Idolatry,'" he proclaimed, his boyish voice just changing so that sometimes it cracked, as he recited from memory, translating from Hebrew into English as he went:

> After their return from the Babylonian exile the Jews
> cried with a loud voice unto the Lord their God.
> What did they say? They said: "Woe, woe! The Spirit
> of Idolatry destroyed the Temple, and burned the
> Sanctuary, and killed all the righteous, and exiled
> Israel from its land, and still he dances among us!
> Why did you give him to us? Was it not in order to
> receive a reward when we overcame him? We want
> neither him nor his reward!" Thereupon a tablet fell
> from the firmament and on it was written, "Truth."

"Picture it! A tablet comes whirling out of the air and lands at their feet, driving itself deep into the ground so that only the top foot or so of the interred stone is visible. On it is written the single word Truth.

"Someone finds the courage to approach the smoking slab, which is still glowing from its descent from heaven. He tugs on it, but the stone is firmly embedded in the hard ground of Israel. Truth, it says.

"What do you make of that?" Joshua challenged the

crowd. No one responded. "The story goes on to say that the people capture the Spirit, but don't know what to do with him. They can't kill him or, as the prophet warns them, the world will end for lack of sexual desire. What must they do? They must let him go but watch him carefully. In the parable, they blind him.

"People want it to be some external force. They want it to be the Communists or the Jews or the blacks or the conservatives or the liberals or the next-door neighbor or the newcomers down the street. They want it to be Klingons or androids or slimy aliens, but, as the parable shows clearly, it is ourselves."

Then Joshua withdrew into the tent to join the vigil with the others, and the crowd settled back to await the next miraculous stranger who could pass the impassable.

Yes, from all over the globe came new arrivals. Every race and every continent were represented. We had our own miniature UN. Our task was simplified, but at the same time we had many preparations to make. Or rather they did, for I was becoming a hanger-on, a useless appendage to the rainbow-hued glory of the Thirty-Six. I didn't think anyone would miss me, so I slipped off to visit my girlfriend Lola Corolla.

Lola and I didn't see each other much, maybe twice a month. She thinks I'm the Peter Pan type who won't grow up. She wanted me to give up the vaude talent angle and be something meaningful like an actuary or a stockbroker. As I wandered through the silent anticipation of a million souls, I wondered what Lola would think of what I'd gotten myself into.

Lola lived on the Upper East Side. I walked across the park, swimming against the tide of humanity rushing to attend the strange events at Sheep Meadow. Lola was a copywriter for a high-powered, fast-paced ad agency; but I had no doubts that within a few years she would be an account manager—she wanted it badly enough.

We had a rule: neither of us would show up unannounced at the other's place. I phoned her from a corner pay phone, watching idly as two cabs jumped the light from opposite directions and collided. The bumpers just touched. The hacks jumped out of their vehicles to argue. On the third ring Lola picked up.

"Yeah?"

"Hi, Lola, it's me, Dexter."

"Hello, stranger."

I tried to read her voice, hearing caution and neutrality in it.

"What's new, Lola?"

"Same old, same old, you know. Make a buck, spend a buck. What about you?"

"Uh, I've been traveling a lot lately. I'd like to tell you about it. You going to be home?"

A long pause. "Sure, come on up. I just made a pot of coffee."

"Great." Lola was one of few Americans who could serve Jamaican Blue Mountain coffee—she had it shipped from Japan, which had bought the whole crop for the next ten years. "I'm in your neighborhood. I'll be right up." As I hung up one of the cabbies slashed the other with a knife, jumped in his car and backed at thirty miles an hour down the avenue. The other one, bleeding from a shoulder wound, pulled a pistol and hopped in his cab to pursue his assailant. If the Thirty-Six were going to save the world, I wished they'd hurry up about it.

Over Lola's delicious brew I recounted my tales of the Thirty-Six. From the balcony of her small ninth-floor apartment on Lexington, you couldn't see the park, only other high-rise apartment buildings, other balconies. Even the sound of a million exhilarated onlookers just blocks away was lost in the buzz and hum of city noises. But every fifteen minutes the agonizingly sweet tone of the shofar entered the room as clearly as if it emanated from the expensive speakers of Lola's home-entertainment unit.

"Listen," I said, as the fluttering diminuendo passed away.

"What do you suppose it all means?" Lola asked.

I realized that I wasn't sure. "At first they talked about a meeting to help themselves work harder—"

"Against evil, you say?" disbelief in her voice.

"Yes. But recently one of them mentioned a judgment."

"Is this some kind of big publicity stunt, Dexter? Come on, you can tell Lola."

"Honestly, no."

"Well, it could be. I could build a campaign around this for several of my clients. What a gimmick! Tents that glow in the dark in Central Park. A line that only goody-goodies can pass through. A smorgasbord of fellow travelers from all nations!"

"Wild, isn't it?" I admitted.

"Beyond belief. Come on, you creep, tell me, what's the schtick?"

"There is none. It's all true."

"And you're not benefiting from this scam in any way, not cut in for a piece of the action or anything?"

"Only as much as anyone else. I hope they succeed."

"It's got to be a scam, it has to be. I mean, it's too perfect."

"I swear to you, it's real."

Lola set down the delft cup she had held in her petite hands. With her black hair and striking blue eyes, to me a fatally attractive combination, she reminded me of a story-book witch—not the good witch or the bad witch but the kind who knows the secrets of men and will not be fooled by them.

"Dexter, now this is important to me. I want to get inside that tent."

"Are you one of the Thirty-Six?" I asked. *You can never be too sure about these things,* I thought.

"You know better than that, baby." She caressed my arm. The tiny hairs there jumped up to meet her touch. "No, I just want to see them for myself."

"I don't know, Lola. They don't seem to have much need for me anymore. My influence is diminishing. Once they find one another, I doubt they'll have any use for me at all."

"How about tonight, then?"

"Sure, why not?"

"Okay, Dex, show me your supernatural friends."

We warmed up the last of the Jamaican and got ourselves together. By one in the morning, we were on our way through the darkened but never dark streets of Manhattan.

I'd never been in Central Park at night before, except in a cab rushing through the drive. There was a predatory, threatening feeling to the empty walks that made me grip Lola's arm tighter as we walked. *We should be hearing the crowd by now,* I thought to myself. I turned to Lola. "Got your watch on, babe?"

"Sure. It's one-fifteen A.M. So?"

"So it's been half an hour, forty-five minutes now, since I heard the horn." I broke into a run, dragging along Lola, who was barely five-three and took little strides.

"Dexter, I can't run this fast," she protested, but at that minute we rounded a last knoll and broke into the open space at Sheep Meadow.

The tent was gone. A team of military and police investigators was going over the flattened grass under the glare of searchlights, while a crowd of a few hundred still lingered nearby.

I ran up to one of the guards ringing the site. "Where? Where have they gone?"

"Damned if I know." He was a young black marine, obviously not inclined to give me much information. But I was a pushy New Yorker.

"They took the tent with them?" I asked.

"The tent took them, if you ask me."

"What? Did it go airborne?" I speculated, visions of flying carpets soaring in my head.

"Nope. It folded up, kind of suddenlike. And it just kept folding and folding, until it folded right away. Damndest magic act I ever saw."

For the second time, I had lost them. I ignored Lola and sat down on the grass of Sheep Meadow, the only natural surface for miles around this penned-in park bounded on all sides by buildings crammed full of people.

Hours ago people had flooded the meadow with their excited presence. Now they had retreated back into their individual apartments, hostile and lonely. The shofar had blown, but the world had not ended. How could I explain to them that all they had heard was only tuneup for the grand symphony to come? Was I sure of that myself? Where had they disappeared to, the Thirty-Six? Would I see them again? They had given my life meaning, and now they were gone. Dew formed on the matted grass where the tent had stood.

18

Hell in a Hand Basket

For a week or so, the sudden appearance and disappearance of the Thirty-Six was front-page, lead-story news. Then, partly because no trace of them could be found, and partly because a rash of ugly news stories broke, public consciousness of the event faded. Tourists still came to Sheep Meadow to goggle at the fading outlines of the ring, and government agents were no doubt analyzing every thread of canvas and speck of sacred dust they could glean from the site; but the trail was growing cold.

I played at being a talent agent again, but my heart wasn't in it. Occasionally a new act would parade into my office and try to raise me out of my lethargy, but singing dogs and bears on stilts no longer thrilled me. I had had a taste of bigger game and was no longer content with small fry.

I took to buying the newspapers from the major cities of the world, those printed in English anyway, scanning them for any tidbit of news that might reveal their whereabouts.

An article in the *Jerusalem Times* gave me a possible lead, though no one else would have spotted the connection. The hottest trouble spot in the world was the Middle East, as it had been on and off since the end of the First World War. Car bombings and retaliatory Israeli air strikes had reached a level of almost daily attack and retribution. It got so that it was difficult to tell for which terrorist brutality the newest raid was recompense.

My tipoff was a story of a hit-and-run ambush on a bus that had been thwarted by "the surprising intervention of three elderly women accompanied by a middle-aged Asian man, who subsequently disappeared after disarming the terrorists." The story went on to state that the four were being sought for questioning by Israeli police.

The description was too accurate to be a mere coincidence. All sorts of questions flared up in my stoked brain. Had all Thirty-Six been found? Why were they in Israel? Of course, the connection to the original Thirty-Six would be strongest there, but why were they still participating in minor, though admirable, interventions when the whole structure of their effort was threatened?

I thought of flying to Tel Aviv, but then I said to myself, *Dexter, you don't need to go flying around. If the Thirty-Six want you, they'll get you. And if you want to see them, you don't need to take a twenty-hour plane flight.*

The few times they had demonstrated their power to me, I had been properly impressed. The Atlantic Ocean and the Mediterranean Sea stood between us, if I was right; but if I was right, any one of them could cross those two bodies of water in a single second, effortlessly. Listlessly I turned back to the business of finding work for the geeks, freaks, and show-business eccentrics.

Days passed without a signal from the Thirty-Six. I entered into negotiations for a theater on Fourteenth Street to stage a big vaude revival. The Spuds would headline. My musician Mr. Declaville was unavailable, having disappeared in the folding tent along with the Thirty-Six; but there was plenty of other talent out there, though none to my knowledge who could match Simon's chops on the shofar, whose final resounding note I expected to hear at any time.

With an eye to budget considerations, I again held auditions in my office, which for a few days had been the spiritual center of the world but was now returned to its former shabby self.

Laboring in anonymity, that's what I was doing. Why, that was a quality of the Thirty-Six. Not that I considered myself in their league, but still no one outside their circle, except Lola, knew of my activities on their behalf—and Lola doubted me.

July had evaporated into August on the steamy streets of Manhattan when I finally received my next visitation from a representative of the Thirty-Six. I had come to appreciate their gentle ersatz humor and was not overly taken aback when my next visitor arrived in the form of a pet act.

You couldn't mistake the sound of this creature coming up my stairs for anything else: it was a horse. The *clip-clop* of its shod feet reverberated on the tin walls. I leaped to the doorway to see what kind of idiot would try to bring a horse up a flight of stairs and was met on the landing by a Mexican gentleman leading the cutest little miniature pony you ever saw.

"Is that thing housebroken?" I asked, remembering the disastrous results the last time I brought animals into a noncircus setting. Of course, those were elephants.

"Naturally, señor. Would you like to see what she does?"

"Do I have any choice?"

The Mexican looked hurt. He was resplendent under an enormous sombrero with bells jingling from its rim, spangles and sequins bedecking both the hat and the quasi-bullfighter's costume he wore, tight vested and short panted. His hair was salt-and-pepper streaked, and he stood no more than five-foot-four, which made him a perfect setpiece for the pony, which could have reached a height of eighteen inches at most.

"This is the most intelligent horse on earth, my friend. You should be glad I have chosen to present her to you and not to some other agent. I understand William Morris is looking for new acts—"

"All right, all right," I said, leading the way into the office. "What can she do?"

"Oh, she is a special horse, Mr. Sinister." When he said my name in his nasal undertones, it truly did sound *sinister*. "A very special horse," he repeated, his eyebrows signaling up and down like semaphore flags.

"All right. What's the trick? Does she count or pick cards or what?"

"She tells the truth."

"A rare talent for any animal. Can you give me a demonstration?"

"Most assuredly." The Mexican, who had yet to tell me his name, bowed low and introduced his horse. "May I present Fonseca the Wise. She is almost one hundred years old, did you know that?"

I did know that ordinary horses live thirty years at most. Still, this was a dwarf. Perhaps her shrunken size elongated her life expectancy.

"A demonstration, Señor—?" I fumbled, not knowing his name.

"Alphonso. Alphonso Diaz, at your service. Ask Miss Fonseca a question, señor. She tells only the truth."

"Yes or no questions only, I suppose?"

"Oh, no, señor, anything you like."

"But how will she answer? I suppose she'll neigh and you'll translate for her?"

Instead of answering, Señor Diaz gestured to the horse. "Ask, Mr. Sinister. Ask for yourself."

I asked for it. I said, *"Como esta usted,* Señorita Fonseca?"

Of course, the horse began to talk, like a low-key Mr. Ed, only sweetly feminine and not so sarcastic. "Very well, thank you."

I watched Señor Diaz while the horse's mouth moved but could detect no twitching of the lips or any other giveaway of ventriloquism. Either the señor was very good or—

"How are you today, Dexter Sinister, human friend of the Thirty-Six?"

Ah so, I thought. And *Touché!* and also *voilà!,* not to mention *Eureka!* Aloud I said, "So, show yourself in human form."

"You are mistaken, Señor Sinister," the horse replied. It was better than talking to ladybugs. "I am a horse. But I am also an acquaintance of the Thirty-Six. They have asked me to assist you in a matter they cannot take care of."

"No problem. Always glad to help." And I was, even if it meant postponing plans for the show opening.

"Fine. Come with me." With that, the tiny pony clattered toward the office door, leading Señor Diaz by the leash end.

"Where are we going?" I asked.

Señor Diaz shrugged his shoulders in the "Que Sera Sera" mode.

I elicited no more stares accompanying a midget horse than midget humans, as we cantered up Eighth Avenue, then through the park, scene of my recent triumph and heartbreak.

We crossed into Lola's neighborhood and continued uptown until we reached the lower Eighties. When Miss Fonseca slowed up in front of the Soviet consulate, I suspected I knew what was coming.

"There's some trouble here that they can't deal with, attend to, is that right?"

"Yes."

"Is there a bomb in one of the cars here?"

"Yes."

"How long do I have?"

The reduction of an equine scratched the ground impatiently with one hoof. "About forty-five seconds now."

I screamed. Then I yelled madly, "Which car? Which car!"

Miss Fonseca trotted back and forth, up and down Eighty-second Street. Apparently her sense of smell wasn't as developed as her vocal abilities.

"This one, I think." She nodded toward a beat-up Chevy Nova parked in a yellow zone on the opposite curb.

"What do I do?" I screeched. The doors and trunk could be booby-trapped. I had no experience with these things. I don't even like firecrackers.

"Relax, Dexter. You only have to cut the red wire. Snip the red wire. Got it?"

I had it. Blindly—without fear for my life, because I thought it was over already—I threw open the passenger door. On the front seat, neatly stowed in a wicker picnic basket, was a menacing bundle of wires and gelatin, pounds of it, like the hideous artificial lard the fast-food chains use in fifty-pound blocks. Oozy petrochemical.

A jumble of wires confronted me, some orange, some sienna, one vaguely red but faded, like a sun-bleached color.

"Which one, which one?" I shouted, but Mr. Alphonso Diaz and his trick horse Fonseca were nowhere in sight.

"Figures," I muttered. I took a best guess and yanked at the nearest wire in the spectrum. It came free in my hand, but I couldn't be sure I'd succeeded until I'd counted a full thirty seconds beyond the forty-five Miss Fonseca had allotted me.

19

Eight-Ninths
Don't Make It

I took a few days off after the bomb incident at the consulate. My hands trembled worse than the day I'd tried to break up the fight on the subway. In the subway I had been able to clown my way out of the situation. This time I'd faced death directly. My general ignorance of all things mechanical had nearly cost me my life. Instead, I was a minor hero. The *Daily News* ran a picture of me shaking hands with the Bomb Squad.

On a Friday morning, I rented a cabin in Amagansett on Long Island, three-fourths of the way out to Montauk. I phoned Lola at work, but she had plans, so I rented a car and drove out there by myself.

The cabin was a place I'd rented several times previously, a delightful gray-shingle, salt-box guest house on the oceanside. The lawn of the cabin ran right into a salty inlet.

An old but serviceable dinghy was tied to an iron ring in the ground, the boat's nose resting on the muddy intersection of lawn and salt water. You could take the boat farther up the inlet and explore the marshes, or you could row toward where the mouth of the inlet opened to the sea.

Swans and mallards used the sheltered waters as a nesting area. The old couple who owned the guest house and a larger home on the property encouraged the waterfowl with daily feedings of stale bread. The honking and quacking was just the soothing natural sound I needed to replace the city's destructive cacophony and ease the unexploded tension of nearly shattered nerves.

Saturday morning I made some coffee and sat in the rowboat without going anywhere. The soft lapping of the changing tide lulled me back toward sleep. The sun rose lazily into a gray sky, the light of Long Island softly diffused over the landscape. I must have lain back at some point, because the next thing I remembered was waking up and looking around to discover that the dinghy had somehow come loose from its mooring and I had drifted out with the tide into open water.

I turned to look for the reassuring presence of the shoreline and discovered none. I was completely at sea. How was that possible? I couldn't have slept so long—it would take quite some time for land to slip beyond the horizon line. I'd have to be over four miles from shore.

Lately, whenever things weren't as they were supposed to be, I was quick to ascribe the aberration to the Thirty-Six. *Let's see, maybe they'll come as a school of dolphin,* I pondered, *or a voluble octopus.* I'd talked to bugs and bonsai equines, why not sea mammals or cephalopods?

The dinghy had oars, and I knew I must be drifting east; so I pointed the prow of the little craft toward the setting sun, hey, I *had* been out all day! I took up the oars and began to row toward the west, not eager to spend a night at sea in my shorts and pajama top, without food or water.

This time my predicament might be my own doing, not the intervention of the Thirty-Six. Had I tied the rope securely after my first boat trip last night?

An hour of strenuous oar work brought me no sight of land. It was nearly twilight. The temperature was dropping, and the late-afternoon breeze had kicked up whitecaps and spray. I rubbed my chafed hands together and splashed some salt water, for that's all there was, on my sunburned face.

What a fool I was! With the fate of the world in the balance, I'd gone off to visit my girlfriend and lost track of the Thirty-Six. Then, just after I had reestablished a shaky connection with them, or at least heard from one of their representatives, I put myself in danger of losing my life before anything could happen. I knew that the current could easily carry me into deep water outside the fishing lanes, and I could die of dehydration and exposure before being rescued.

Morning found me still adrift. Blisters had formed on my hands, and my throat was raw and painful. I may have been a little delirious when the first noisy flock of Canadian geese passed overhead. Idly I counted—nine, ten, twelve.

A second flight followed the first. Another twelve in another perfect V-shaped formation. They were high up, but I was pretty sure they were geese. Faintly I heard their mellifluous calls to one another as they flew.

A third group trailed the first two. Six, seven, eight this time. As I watched, the last goose peeled off from the flock and spiraled slowly down toward me. Coming out of the east, it was silhouetted in the morning sun, its magnificent wingspan straining in a steep dive, its graceful neck arched fiercely. I thought it was going to dive-bomb me when it pulled up in a flutter of feathers, walked on water for a few yards, and tumbled into my boat.

The transformation was abrupt, but I managed to get a quick glimpse of the incredible molting that occurred while this forlorn goose metamorphosed into Mr. Chin, retiring Asian gentleman.

"Please excuse the inconvenience of this meeting place, Mr. Sinister," he began by way of explanation, "but since our coming out in New York, we have had to be more circumspect."

"That—" I said, pointing to the sky, "those are you?"

"Yes. Quite a sight, eh?"

"You'd better watch out for hunters. It's not duck season yet, and Canadian geese are protected, but there are always poachers."

"Thank you for your concern, but birdshot will not harm us."

"I counted only thirty-two."

"Exactly. The very reason I have come to see you, Mr. Sinister. It would appear that there are some parts of the world so remote that the people there have not heard our message. We remain four short of our total."

"Can't you—I mean, aren't thirty-two of you enough?"

"Sadly, no. Remember that the original reason for our convocation is that all Thirty-Six have not been enough of late."

"Mmmmm."

"Help us find them, Mr. Sinister. Time grows short."

"Of course."

"And now, I must return to the flock. Good day, Mr. Sinister."

"Hey, wait!" I shouted, as Mr. Chin rose out of the dinghy and reemerged as a flying fowl. "Help me! I'll die out here!" But the bird was already cresting the wind and sweeping west on outstretched wings.

The wind rose and the waves piled up on one another until I was seasick from the tempestuous rocking. But I could feel the little boat being rushed along toward the west by the foaming sea, and in a few minutes the twinkling morning star of the lighthouse at Montauk Point came into view. A last gust of wind, like an unseen hand, pushed me into the shallows of Amagansett. I tore my pajama top in half, wrapped the cloth around my injured hands, and rowed home.

20

Unknown in Nome

Instead of having a restful weekend in the country, I nearly died. Instead of being able to forget my problems, I was led to sea and dive-bombed by one of the Thirty-Six.

How do I search for four anonymous individuals so isolated, so removed from modern communications technology that they hadn't heard of the first convocation of the Thirty-Six?

Where are the most remote regions of the earth? The poles, the deserts, the high mountains, the Arctic tundra, tiny islands in the open ocean. Except for the poles, all are inhabited—the task was impossible. I could only hope for blind luck and synchronicity—that I would be in the right place at the right time because I was meant to be there.

I mean, one of the four could be an unknown in Nome. No, hell, Nome was a metropolis compared to the lonely outposts I was likely to locate the final four, as I thought of them, being an old college basketball fan.

I had to start somewhere, so I chose the wilds of Alaska. Nome had entered my head. It was a good jumping-off point for my absurd, clueless hunt for elusive quarry. It was a one-in-a-million shot, or rather four-in-five-billion, but what else was I to do?

In fourteen hours I had gone from the international madness of Kennedy Airport to the icy tarmac at Nome International, where you deboard your plane down a shaky metal staircase and cross the wind-whipped open to enter a terminal reminiscent of a train station.

I'd outfitted myself in L.L. Bean's finest and looked like a regular tourist moose hunter, except that I carried no vinyl shotgun case.

Before I'd left the office I'd booked a guide who could take me to the string of Eskimo villages along the Bering Strait west of Nome. My travel agent, Stanley, whom I had finally forgiven and let back into my good graces, had assured me that he knew the real McCoy.

So now I stood among the eclectic population of Alaska —part Indian, part pioneer, and part recent arrival—a mixed bag of oil roughnecks, townspeople, and shaggy, bearded, shifty-eyed backcountry types. At the airport things were a little more normal than I could expect in town; after all, airports tend to draw a better sort of crowd. I looked around for my guide, hoping it wasn't the Gabby Hayes lookalike wearing the foxskin cap with the tail down the back Davy Crockett style. It was.

The rest of his outfit was equally outlandish. He wore outsized mukluks so large they looked like hip boots on him, and a lumberjack's shirt that couldn't have left L.L. Bean's much before my shiny new gear. He strode right up to me and confirmed my fears.

"Sinister. Fess Festinger's the name," he said, pronouncing it the French-Canadian way with a soft *g* and the accent on the last syllable. "Welcome to Nome, stinkhole of the North. Let's clear out of this joint before I get the city jitters."

"How did you identify me?" I asked.

"You were the only New Yorker who got off the plane."

"How do you know I'm a New Yorker?"

"Still got the *New York Post* sticking out of the pocket on your flight bag."

A tracker, I thought, *a regular big-game hunter's guide. Spots all the clues.* He'd clean up in my business. I examined him again. The shirt might be new, but the rest of him was as grizzled as the stubby beard he wore. He was the real thing, as Stanley had promised, an old-time trapper who now made his living off tourists of one kind or another.

"Where's your rifles?" he asked.

I hadn't told him what game it was I was after. "I'm not here for shooting," I said.

"Ahh. You another one of those pansy photographers?"

"Nope. I want to meet the people in the smallest, farthest-out villages you can take me to."

"What are you, an anthropologist type? I've had a few of those come through here, and I can tell you, the Eskimo elders don't like you messing with their cultures—"

"No, I'm not one of them. I just want to talk. Call it a hobby."

"Sure. Whatever, as long as your money's good. Let's go."

We drove out of Nome in his beat-up pickup on an unpaved road that ended at an encampment on the edge of the Bering Sea. The brief Alaskan summer had just ended, and ice floes were beginning to pile up again along the coast. By winter you wouldn't be able to tell snow-covered land from ice-covered sea, but now we could still safely trek north toward the Eskimo villages where I had a crazy, vague premonition or hope or hunch that I might find number thirty-three. We reached the village after a day's walk on snowshoes.

"If you think you're going to find a tribe of innocents out here, you're way off the trail, Sinister. These folks are welfare loafers, living off the government dole. Half of 'em are AA members and the other half should be. They have rustic-looking log cabins and still kill caribou for food, but they sit at home at night and get drunk to watch fifties reruns on Nome television, just like everybody else."

"I wish I'd known that before I started this hike, pal," I said, disappointment worsening the ache in my calves from the heavy footgear. What was I doing out here if these people had satellite dishes and cable TV? "I suppose you heard about the big doings in New York last week?" I asked.

"Oh, hell yeah. We got pictures of the crowds, but you couldn't really see much. Most people here think the whole thing was fake."

"It wasn't, believe me. So, everyone here in these villages has seen and heard about it?"

"Probably. What's the connection?"

"You wouldn't understand," I said, still not crediting the old guy enough for his perspicacity.

"I might," he answered. We entered the first village, a collection of ten randomly scattered log huts set in mud. A satellite dish penned in by a tumbledown wooden fence was the centerpiece of the village, which sat on a small knoll above a bay. Shy children and mothers peered at us from doorways. The sharp tangy smell of salted fish permeated the air.

"Are all the villages like this?"

"Yup," Fess Festinger said.

"All right, let's go back."

"Too late today for that. Just what were you expecting? What did you want, anyhow?" he asked.

"You wouldn't believe me if I told you."

"You're looking for a wise man, is that it?" He had put the pieces together for himself and was only looking for confirmation.

"That's right."

"Somebody who hasn't heard the news about what happened in New York, but maybe should have?"

"That's it."

"Why didn't you say so? I know someone who might fill the bill, but she's not in any of these villages."

"Where then?"

"She's in a nursing home in Nome. Doesn't watch TV, says it tries to capture her soul. She keeps trying to sneak out to the tundra to die, but they won't let her. That's the Eskimo way, you know, to take your grandmother out and leave her to freeze when she decides it's time. Quite a humane and gentle way to go. I've been close to it myself a few times. You just slip right off, peacefullike."

He rattled on, but I could only think, *Nome, Nome, Nome.* How had I known?

We spent the night in the village of Katchinchinook, watching TV and drinking with the village elders. Riots had broken out in Detroit, Memphis, Miami, and elsewhere. Three South American democracies had been toppled by military coups. Tensions were rising all over the globe. After the episode of the tent in Central Park, a cult of Thirty-Six worshipers had sprung up, and their followers were being detained and tortured in a dozen countries. This was a new development I wasn't prepared for and didn't know how to deal with. Should I contact them? Sitting in the rank smokiness of an Eskimo cabin on the edge of a cold northern sea, I felt far removed from the horrific events pouring from the tube. I wanted to ask the elders how they felt about all this, but they quickly got too drunk for any meaningful discussion. Their Al-Anon wives resignedly trundled them off, and we were left to chew on the stringy elk jerky that, with salty fish, was their main sustenance, washed down with some warm Wild Turkey.

The next morning we trekked back over the frozen wild, picked up our truck, and returned to Nome. The nursing home accepted visitors only in the morning; so it was not until the next day that I was able to meet Miss Betty.

Because I had called ahead, she had been informed by the staff that she was going to have visitors. One always fears the worst going to visit an elderly person confined to a convalescent home, but Miss Betty turned out to be a cheerful, active woman who spent most of her day strolling the grounds, bundled up in a woven shawl but far more interested in life than most of her compatriots, who remained indoors with the television and endless bingo and card games as their only diversions. She greeted us vibrantly on the front steps of the home and asked us to join her for her morning constitutional.

The people at the home called her Miss Betty because they didn't know, and she wouldn't tell them, her real Eskimo name. She'd been brought to them because all of her sons and grandsons had up and died on her.

Fess had traded skins and supplies with her when she was matriarch of a whole clan on a stretch of coast that the government later annexed, displacing her and her people to a new settlement nearer Nome that was not nearly so conducive to their way of life. In recompense, the government gave them money and introduced them to the destructive pleasures of alcohol.

"So," I said, as we walked the rocky path around the home, "Fess tells me you don't like television."

"Young man, next to alcohol, television is the worst destroyer of Eskimo brains there is. Bad for you. Eats up your mind. In Inuit we call it gangattaqitausimajug."

"You haven't heard much world news recently, then?" I said cautiously.

"The world. They took my whole big world away and gave me a room in there"—she gestured to the dingy, unappealing boardinghouse structure, low and plain—"to replace it. You know, I used to walk thirty miles between villages, in blizzards, and think nothing of it." I knew that, unlike Fess Festinger, she was not bragging.

I looked down at this feisty, wrinkled little character in her colorful Eskimo clothing, wondering if I could somehow close the gap between us. "Mr. Festinger here says you're an a'kulag'uluk, a wise one. Is that so?"

"Mr. Festinger is a fool."

Fess spit on the pebbly path but said nothing.

"Be that as it may," I went on, "I'm here for a special reason. There's a group of—a group, some people, who—" I stumbled, not knowing how to proceed.

She made it easy for me. "Who love the world so much, they would have it be as it used to be, in harmony."

"Yes."

She needed say no more. I knew that I had found my unknown in Nome, and I promised to follow all hunches, wherever they might lead.

"Take me to them," Miss Betty said, and I saw that she was crying for joy. What a lonely struggle it must have been for her, always giving to the world and being repaid with cruelty, deception, and defeat. Now, at the end of her life, when she might have died lonely and alone, she would join her fellows in a final cathartic upheaval. Having heard her plaintive words, now more than ever I feared the judgment of the just.

21

Spuds Rule

The world sank further and further into the abyss. The stock market dove and the price of gold rose, predictably, though what people thought they were going to be able to do with all those Krugerrands was beyond me. No one could predict the future with any confidence.

For myself, I withdrew further into the innocent fantasy of my brand of entertainment. It was easy to slip into reveries of nostalgia—the present was so distasteful, and finding Miss Betty had been so exhausting.

When I returned to New York with Miss Betty, I found Mr. Chin—once again *Homo sapiens* and not avian—ensconced in my office. I didn't even bother to ask him how he got into my office; I just left Miss Betty in his charge.

Tired from my trek on the tundra, I wanted a little time off, so I booked shows and went about my business. I felt it just wasn't possible to be on the road continuously in search of the last of the Thirty-Six.

It was time for the Fordham Follies—an annual charity gig at Fordham University. The kids liked noisy, showy stuff—rock bands—but if you were sly, you could slip them some magic or acrobatics as a warmup act without losing them. Something made me think of The Spuds.

I phoned the Park Plaza, but they had no record of seven midget jugglers staying there. Last time I'd made the mistake of looking for them in the midnight-cowboy hotels in Times Square and the Bowery. This time I concentrated on the nicer joints and found them on the fifth try at the Commodore.

"Fred, baby, how's things?"

"Who's this?" Fred shot back.

"It's your favorite booking agent, Dexter Sinister. How's Chuckie and Fahey and Little Bob and the guys?"

"Sinister. Hmmph!" A silence followed.

"What's the matter, Freddy?"

"We're busy, Sinister. We don't have time for entertaining some old geezers on a cruise ship—"

"This is a one-nighter, Fred. The Fordham Follies. A bunch of college kids. You'll wow 'em."

"I don't know, Sinister. We're busy."

"With what?" I asked, half a dozen smart-alec remarks on the tip of my tongue.

"With the job you should be doing!" Fred let me have it.

I was floored. What could he be talking about? During the week on the ship, none of the midgets hinted at knowing of the existence of the Thirty-Six, revealed to me on that voyage.

Cautiously I inquired: "Just what are you referring to, Fred?"

"You really want to know? Come down to the Commodore this afternoon." Then he hung up on me.

Curious, and still hopeful of signing them for the Follies, I showed up that afternoon at the Commodore and took the elevator up to their suite just in time to turn around and accompany them back down to the lobby and out onto Forty-second Street. We hailed a cab. Once we were settled in, Fred turned his hard face to me, a mean little face that didn't jibe with the offhand remark he'd made this morning implying some connection with my holy crew. Fred seemed to read my mind, because he snapped off a comeback to my unuttered impression.

"Don't judge a book by its cover, Sinister. I got connections with people in high places, follow me?"

I thought I did.

We crossed into Brooklyn and entered a section of town I personally avoided, passing under it many times on the way to Far Rockaway without ever once having gotten off. It didn't even have a name, this part of town; though vaguely close to Flatbush and Atlantic, it was eons and parasangs removed from that richly ethnic corner. Burned-out automobiles littered the sides of the street. Rows of fading red-brick tenements comprised the housing, like those in Manhattan before the gentrification and the construction of high-rise project housing. Prostitutes and drug dealers, a mixture of Latin, black, and white, loitered at the corners and in doorways. I was nervous even inside the cab, and when Fred told the cabbie to pull over, I really got shaky; but I was not as scared as the hack, who locked the doors, turned on his Off-Duty sign, and sped out of the area as soon as we were out of his cab.

"What are we doing in this neighborhood, Fred?" I asked.

"Charity work, just like you do," said Fred.

The Spuds walked single file down the street, which only increased their resemblance to the Seven Dwarfs. Just about that time I heard gunshots from around the corner, unmistakable little spitting sounds. The Spuds broke into a trot, fanning out until they were in a line, running down the street as if in a miniature football formation.

It was an exhibition of naked bravery such as one usually sees only in wartime. Around the corner came two men in ski masks, each one clutching a bulky flight bag and a gun. The flying wedge of unarmed Spuds cut the fleeing men's feet out from under them. Both men got off a wild shot before being overwhelmed by superior numbers of muscular arms and legs—four-to-one against one guy, and three-to-one against the other. Within seconds both were subdued and quickly tied up. I stood on a streetcorner and watched. Fred left the mopping up to the others and approached me with a scornful look.

"Thanks for pitching in, Sinister."

"You didn't need any help, Fred. Anyway, I can't see how protecting banks is charity work."

"They didn't rob a bank, moron. There's no money in those bags."

I had blithely assumed there was. "What, then?"

"There's fifty pounds of pure heroin in each bag. They just ripped off another dealer who lives in a row house over there—probably blew him away." Fred gestured around the corner, where police cars were pulling up, sirens wailing.

"Why not just let them do one another in for it?" I asked, humane sort that I am.

"The dope's bad. Would have killed half the junkies in New York City if it made the street."

"Ah." All I could say was, "Ah." It seemed that I really was in touch with a high moral order, one that would deem the saving of the lives of heroin addicts as worth risking their own lives for. Fred, and all The Spuds, grew tall in my estimation. Never again would I make fun of them. They were heroes.

"Now, does that give you some impetus to get off your duff and get busy with your task?"

"Yes, sir."

"Okay. How much you offering us for the Fordham Follies gig?"

I had many questions to ask Fred—which of the Thirty-Six contacted him? Was it one I had already found? As we walked to a subway stop—no cabs would intentionally venture into this neighborhood unless they had to, so hailing one was out of the question—I asked Fred about his relationship to the Thirty-Six; but he would only say that I had already learned my lesson for the day.

In the morning I would renew my search. How could I slack off, when men such as these were standing up for the Thirty-Six?

22

The Women Jugglers
of Tonga

Even though I'd found Miss Betty in Nome instead of out on the frozen tundra, I still hadn't given up on the "remote corners of the earth" angle. After my experience with The Spuds redirected me, I saw an opportunity to combine the hunt for the last three members of the Thirty-Six with my talent business, to my advantage for a change, though why I still thought it important to keep up the agency was hard to understand, since I of all people should realize that if things didn't change, pretty soon there would be no business.

I guess it was force of habit, the feeling that I ought to go to work, even if the end was near. Anyway, I had always heard stories about the fabled islands of Tonga, where it was rumored among jugglers that every woman on the islands could juggle at least five items at a time.

Among jugglers, five is the magic number that separates your ordinary, run-of-the-mill street juggler from the real professional. To juggle five balls, you have to be able to perform an endless series of three-ball flashes, all balls in the air for enough time to clap your hands in between. The space where you clap is where the extra two balls go. The thought of an entire female population able to routinely perform this difficult a feat was intriguing.

I examined Tonga's position on the map and saw that it was almost two thousand miles from anywhere in the far-thest remote corner of the South Pacific—far from Austra-lia, far from Hawaii, far from the Philippines or the Asian mainland. It was perfect.

I quickly learned that Tonga was made up of over one hundred small islands, and that only the main island of Nuku'alofa was even vaguely equipped with twentieth-cen-tury devices. I could wander for years among the tiny coral reefs that constituted the rest of the Tongan archipelago, searching for one lost man or woman. But at least I would see the women jugglers for myself, or put to bed a quirky legend.

I headed right out to Kennedy Airport and took a four-teen-hour, uncomfortably bumpy jet ride to Fiji, the nearest island with an airport of any size.

From Fiji I transferred into a smaller jet and flew the rest of the way to Tonga. Within the space of forty-eight hours I had traversed six of the world's seven temperate zones, crossed the international date line, and traveled well over ten thousand miles. I collapsed in a rented beach bungalow without so much as looking at the Pacific and slept for two days.

When I finally ventured out into the streets of Nuku'alofa, I found a colonial city of whitewashed build-ings run from an elegant British house by a benevolent and charmingly anachronistic royalty. I also found beautiful white sand beaches and lovely maidens, an incipient horde of tourists, but no female jugglers. I stopped at the local tourist information center and inquired. Yes, they told me, there were islands where juggling was still a part of the local culture, but many were restricted so as to preserve the native culture.

I was also told there were holy men in Tonga; they resided on those same proscribed islands. If I made application to visit them, I would be approved by the proper authorities within the next year or two.

I retreated to my bungalow to plan strategy.

After coming all this way, I could hardly turn around and return to New York without some effort to make contact. Somewhere out there among the millions of square miles of salt water, on a sandy beach beneath coconut palms, I was sure one of the last three Thirty-Sixers awaited me, perhaps even now staring at the blank horizon, wondering who was going to come and get him or her. I couldn't let them down.

I wandered down to the docks at the harbor, to the section where the giant catamarans and oceangoing yachts berthed. It was a Saturday afternoon. Deck parties and bikinis abounded. Dark flesh was all around, some natural, some tanned, all alluring. The tropical drowsiness of a hot late afternoon was almost palpable.

Venturing onto the floating dock planks, I approached one less elegant-looking hull, a wooden Dutch gaff-rigged boat far from the canals of Holland where she'd been launched. A blond sailor in cutoffs and a T-shirt, white cream crowning his nose, lazily hosed fresh water onto teak deck slats.

"Any boats for hire out here?" I asked.

The blond's equally bronzed and blond girlfriend raised her head to check out the stranger from her prone position on a webbed hammock hung from the bowsprit.

"For sure. Where ya wanna go?" My harsh New York accent collided in the air with his bland California slang.

"One of the off-islands. I want to see some women jugglers."

"Neat. Only, you aren't allowed to go there, right?"

"Right."

"I'll take ya."

"Great," I said. "When?"

"How about right now?"

Why not? I thought and hoisted myself heavily on board.

"Can you sail?" he asked.

I can, but with my last sea trip in the dinghy in mind and my hands not completely healed, I begged off.

Donny, as he introduced himself, had to rouse Diane from the hammock to play first mate and trim the jib.

We motored out of the harbor, hoisted sail, and were soon heeled over nicely on a long starboard tack. I took a look down below and found a paneled cabin with everything stowed neatly away as it should be on a good sailboat. A little potbellied woodstove was a surprising fixture, as was the oriental carpet on the cabin floor. Whoever these people were, they lived in style.

"So, 'what's it all about, Alfie?'" Diane cooed to me when we were well under way.

"What do you mean?" I said.

"Hey, man, everybody's got an angle. What's yours?"

"I told you," I answered, exasperated at the Californians' thickheadedness. "I'm looking for women jugglers."

"Yeah," the blond sailor retorted. "You said that. What for? You need an agile wife or something?"

"I'm a variety talent agent. They sound like a novelty. That's all." These two were making me uneasy with their insinuating questions. I began to think they suspected me of being a drug dealer or a white slaver or a buyer of exotic, perhaps endangered and protected animals. Or maybe they were one of the above. I felt vulnerable aboard their boat. Who were they, anyway? I hadn't checked them out with the authorities; I'd just hopped on and sailed away. They hadn't even asked for money—yet.

The afternoon dragged on into an ocher sunset, incinerating everything to the horizon in great flames of light. The sailboat cleft to its tack. Donny and Diane took turns at the helm for a while, then Diane disappeared below decks for some time.

When she emerged, she had changed from her bathing suit into white slacks and a tanktop, and she had fixed a light dinner for the three of us. Donny uncorked a bottle of wine, and suddenly the couple didn't seem so mysterious or threatening.

We toasted the venture, and toasted again. The sailboat knifed quietly into the twilight, a watery plain more vast than either the Maine potato field or even the table-flat Alaskan tundra I'd recently visited.

"So, Dexter," Diane started in again, when she felt that I was sufficiently mellow, "what *really* brings you to Tonga?"

"I told you—"

"Don't give us that women juggler crap," Diane cut me off. "We know a hustler when we see one. Hey, it's okay —you're with modern pirates, baby. This is what we do, these backdoor trips. You found the right folks."

Now I was truly frightened. There was no telling what these two were capable of doing. I decided to take a wild gamble and tell them the true story of my quest.

"Have you ever heard the Jewish folktale of the Thirty-Six Just Men?" I asked. By their bored and indolent stares I could see that they had not. I launched into my tale, including a description of the flying women, Mr. Chin as a Branta Canadensis, my connection with the goings-on in Central Park (of which they had heard but little), and so forth. They listened with some interest to my tale. When I stumbled to a finish, there was a moment of silence.

"So," Diane asked, "what for?"

"Huh?"

"What are you helping them for? Have they promised you anything?"

"Only to save the world."

"No, I mean you personally?"

"No."

"I only know one other person who thinks like you, and we're headed toward his island right now."

"Fabulous." My luck had held. "What's his name?"

"Na'huatl. You'll have to introduce yourself. We don't actually know him; we've only heard of him. He don't truck with people like us."

"Tell me what you know."

"Na'huatl is the chief on the island we're going to, and he's the one who's lobbied the big island for many years to keep all the tourists and good old entrepreneurs like us off his land. But he's not warlike. If you come messing with him, he runs you off, but he doesn't kill you and eat you, like some of his tribesmen might want to do. Actually I've got a lot of respect for him. So much respect I'm going to drop anchor about half a mile offshore and let you take the dinghy in. But don't think you're going to be able to talk him into leaving or anything like that. He's devoted to his people and this island. He'll never leave."

"Let me meet him first, then we'll see."

We sailed all night. Morning found us bobbing just beyond the breakers of a coral island. Donny and Diane lowered their wooden dinghy into the water and passed me a set of undersized, plastic oars. As I was fitting the oars into the oarlocks, I noticed Donny hoisting the main sail. *That's an odd thing to do at anchor*, I thought; but then I saw that they weren't at anchor anymore. As soon as I was safely in the dinghy, Diane had hauled up, and they were gradually drifting away as they caught the breeze, while I was being pulled toward the shore by the rolling ocean swells.

"Hey!" I yelled. "Where are you going?"

"Big island."

"Why?"

"First off, you're crazy. Also, we don't want Na'huatl to catch us. I lied," Diane yelled. "He does eat people. You'll be perfect for each other."

"What about the dinghy?" I shouted.

"Keep it!" came the distant response, for they were already leaning into a beam reach away from me.

There was nothing to do but paddle toward shore and a Tongan chief who either was or wasn't anthropophagic.

Now, I'm no anthropologist, and I don't know if Tonga does or doesn't have a history of cannibalism; but short of drifting around the South Pacific 'til I met the fate I barely escaped off Long Island, I didn't have much choice except to beach the dinghy and face the music. Dimly I became aware of a Valkyric chorus of human voices that soared over the insistent drumming of the combers.

Was I hallucinating? I scuffed the boat bottom onto glistening sand and hopped out. No, there it was again, an angelic sound, a cappella voices raised in hymn. A broad path through giant banyan trees led me to a plain white New England clapboard church, apparently dropped from the sky onto this tropical island. Its spire was topped with a modest cross, just as it would be in rural Vermont.

The church burst with song, spilling music out onto the hot Tongan landscape like a cool liquid. I recognized an archaic plainsong from a hymnal no longer in use in American churches. Without instrumentation, with only their voices to carry them, the congregation was spouting eight-part harmony. They finished with a glorious lingering

"Amen" that traipsed up and down the scale before harmonizing and resolving in perfect union.

Apparently that was the closing hymn, for in the next moment the doors flew open and the residents of this island poured out of the church, talking and laughing, some still humming snatches of the last song. No one gave the slightest notice to the stranger dallying by the nearest coconut palm. Certainly none of them eyed me with anything resembling voraciousness.

Last out of the church was an enormous brown man in ecclesiastical garments. He was wearing a bishop's miter that made him seem even taller than his already imposing height. Without a doubt, this was Na'huatl. I approached him, but I didn't know whether to call him Chief or Your Grace, or however it is a lay person should address a bishop. Fortunately for me, he spoke first.

"Leave this island at once." His cheerfully corpulent face struggled to take on a sternness that it seemed incapable of displaying.

Seeing this, I became bold. "Your reverence," I addressed him, taking my best shot at an honorific, "I mean no harm. I'm not here for profit or plunder. I come as a representative of a peace group—"

"You can stop right there," Na'huatl interrupted me. "I have already declared these islands a nuclear-free zone. We need no help from outsiders to keep the bomb tests from our area."

"That is a grave threat," I agreed. We stood outside the little church in the blazing sunlight. I was sweating heavily; the three-hundred-pound bishop was cool. "But the group I am an agent for is concerned with a larger issue than nuclear test bans or even nuclear war."

"Now what could that be?" Na'huatl said with a slight smile. Whether he found it amusing that there could be a greater threat than nuclear holocaust, or for some other reason, I could not tell.

"These people believe that—that the world depends on them, and that their best efforts are failing. Does any of this make sense to you?"

The chief suddenly went pale, or as pale as a sun-darkened brown man can go.

"In some ways I had hoped you would never come," he said.

"Why do you say that?"

"Would you want to leave if this were your home?" He gestured to the paradise that surrounded us, the peaceful environment that was his domain and had been his family's home for as long as anyone could remember.

"I thought you were supposed to be unknowns, simple folk. Here you are a tribal chief and a bishop—"

"I'm neither. I just like the hat. And our people have no chief, though I suppose they look to me for some decisions. Want to know my business—I'm a banana farmer. Is that simple enough?"

"One other thing," I said, wanting to cover all the bases, "the people who brought me out here suggested . . . I'm sorry to bring this up, but they suggested—you were cannibalistic."

"Can you think of a better rumor to scare off nosy unwanted visitors?"

I could not. "They left me without transportation. How are we going to get to Nuku'alofa?"

"I have a way," Na'huatl replied.

"Oh, do you fly or turn into a bird, too?"

The great chief and thirty-fourth of the Thirty-Six looked at me strangely. "I have a boat."

I never did see any women jugglers.

23

Quiet Time in the Gooney Colony

I hadn't been doing this on my own, I realized, as I dozed on the plane flight back to New York. I hadn't been alone. The Thirty-Six had been guiding my thoughts and actions. "The last few will be easier to locate," Mr. Chin had said.

Na'huatl's bulk required him to buy two seats, but money seemed to be no problem to him, and his passport was in order. He attracted considerable attention from the other passengers, but only as a primitive curiosity. None of them understood as I did that they were flying with one of the world's true marvels. Perfectly at ease, Na'huatl bantered with his admirers while I tried to avoid jet lag with fitful naps.

We arrived, passed through customs without incident, and clambered into a taxi. The dispatcher let two parties get ahead of us in line to make sure that Na'huatl was transported in a big boxy Checker cab that could hold him.

For the first time I saw the Tongan's face darken as we passed through some of the high-rise neighborhoods of outer Queens. "People should not live on top of one another," he said with conviction.

How could I explain to him that these were desirable areas of the city, Kew Gardens and the like.

It got worse as we entered the boiling caldron of cars and trucks that poured into Manhattan through the tunnel. Trapped in the poorly lit, smelly subterranean tube, we crawled along for half an hour. I thought I was going to lose the chief right then and there, as his face blackened and he swooned from the fouled air. When we emerged onto the congested intersection of Thirty-second Street and First Avenue—horns going off all around us, cabbies battling for the last inch of available roadway, pedestrians risking their lives to cross against the light—I thought Na'huatl was going to cry, so troubled were the lines of his face.

"Only a few blocks across town to my office, Chief."

What Hell have you brought me to? his eyes seemed to ask, but he said nothing. At Times Square, just a block from our destination, at the end of a trip of many thousands of miles, Na'huatl suddenly opened the door at a red light and got out, hoisting the battered steamer trunk that was his only luggage onto his broad back. He signaled me wordlessly that this was goodbye. I understood that the Thirty-Six no longer used my office, or even fit in my office, since there were now thirty-four of them, but somehow his abrupt departure unnerved me. I looked through the back window of the cab as we pulled away through the square and saw the Tongan patriarch seated dismally on his trunk while the dangerous deluge of urban life eddied and swirled around him. I could only hope and assume that his size would discourage muggers and that the other Thirty-Sixers would enfold him into them soon.

Sure enough, on my answering machine when I reached the office was a taped message from Mr. Chin, thanking me for my safe transport of Na'huatl and reminding me that two more remained to be found. I also found an envelope on my desk containing a newspaper clipping that was obviously meant to be my next lead.

It was a wire story about a naturalist, a man who had lived for the past thirty years on a bird sanctuary in the Midway Island chain, studying the habits of the black-footed albatross—the gooney bird. Midway! The South Pacific? I'd just spent eighteen wearying hours on a plane winging away from there. The very thought of yet another long jet trip exhausted me.

I read the rest of the article, which compared the birdman to St. Francis of Assisi in the tenderness and intimacy of his relations with the creatures of the air. The final lines noted that he had left the sanctuary for the first time in many years to travel to—Hosanna in the highest!—Philadelphia to give a speech and accept an award from an ornithologists' group. My travel miles had just been cut from several thousand to ninety.

Birdwatchers of the World had been trying to lure Bill Grebec from his isolation for several years, I learned. The convention was a sellout because of his surprising last-minute acceptance. His speech was scheduled for the next day. I took the Metroliner in the morning and arrived an hour before his speech. The convention was held at the Polish-American Veterans Hall in the heart of working-class Philly. Birdwatchers of all ages crowded into the exhibit hall. Wildlife conservation groups sold memberships, buttons, T-shirts, and the like from rows of booths. A man dressed as a giant condor paraded around the convention center as the official mascot of the gathering. At one end of the hall, several hundred folding chairs were lined up in front of a portable stage, as yet empty save for a flimsy rented podium.

I perused the various slide shows, photo exhibits, and specimen collections. I listened to the cassette recordings and read the literature—all the while feeling a bit like a fox in the chicken coop, for though I loved birds, today I was a hunter after game and would take it on the wing if I had to.

Soon a public-address announcement called the conventioneers to their seats. I noticed that the group was predominantly middle-aged and up, and mostly female. *Well*, I thought, *you can't expect to find Pentagon generals out birdwatching*. In my limited research, however, I had discovered that the armed forces did have an interest in the black-footed albatross, the subject of Bill Grebec's speech, since the birds kept getting sucked into the exhaust of Midway jets. The problem had grown to such proportions that the air force was forced to make a bird sweep before each jet's takeoff to clear the runway of gooney birds. The birds needed a long runway themselves for their own ungainly takeoffs, and the air force runway was perfect for them.

When Bill Grebec took the stage, to me he resembled the gooneys he studied: splayed feet too large for his body, spindly legs too thin for it, a beaked nose, and plumped chest, altogether awkward and comically homely. Of course, he never had the opportunity to spread his wings in graceful flight as the albatrosses did. Unless—unless he was a Thirty-Sixer.

After long-winded and silly introductions by several officials of Birdwatchers of the World, Mr. Grebec seesawed to the podium on stiltlike extremities. He looked like a man who'd been at sea too long and couldn't find his land legs.

"Good morning, birdwatchers," he began. "I come before you for the first and last time, and I am not a natural speechmaker, so forgive me if this is not the most exciting talk you've ever heard."

He needn't have been so modest. For the next half-hour he held us all entranced with his affectionate descriptions of life and love in the gooney colony. I got the distinct impression that he thought of himself as a bird, so closely had his life become entwined with his subjects' lives. He told of their romances; the daily rhythms of their existence; their extraordinarily complex life cycle; their long migrations, during which, after a period of growth on land, they take off and remain airborne for up to seven years.

"Think of it," he said dreamily. "Imagine seven years in the air."

Having just spent eighteen unpleasant hours aloft, I had a hard time getting into the romance of flight, but he won even me over with his lyric recitation.

"Seven years of weightless buoyancy, riding the thermal currents and coasting on the trade winds, never feeling the sagging down-pull of gravity. Hour after hour, day after day, month after month, skimming the ocean, not once touching rude earth.

"Many of you have been to rookeries and other bird colonies and have perhaps witnessed the noisy confusion that bird society can be. But there can also be deep silence and harmony when it's quiet time in the gooney colony, forty or fifty thousand of these great birds at rest. Would that men could emulate these gentle beings and live so peacefully."

At these words my fox ears perked up. Was Bill Grebec hinting at a far more significant role he had played than hermetic naturalist?

When he drew to a close, the moderator asked for questions from the floor. I saw my opportunity. After a couple of innocuous queries about gooney feeding habits, I stood and raised my hand.

"Mr. Grebec," I called out, "you said before that you

wished men could live as peacefully as birds. I take it you
seek to learn from them, and you suggest that we all could
do so. My question is, just how can you apply this knowledge, if you remain alone, away from all human interac-
tion?"

"I could not. You are right. But I have always found
human beings too cruel, too intrusive, too . . . too earth-
bound. I love my fellow men, but I find their company
distressing."

I followed up with a second question, as heads turned in
the front rows to get a look at me. "What has made you
leave the colony at this time? Did you hear the call?"

"I heard." Mr. Grebec flapped his arms peculiarly, as if
agitated. Of all those present, only I guessed correctly what
would happen next. He looked for all the world like a
molting adolescent gooney about to try his wings for the
first time. Without actually changing into a gooney bird, he
was becoming one nonetheless.

"Your companions await you," I said, confident that I
had found my man. At those words Grebec lifted off the
stage once, fluttered uncertainly back down, then stretched
and squawked and ran across the open platform, legs
pumping as he desperately sought sufficient takeoff speed.
At the platform's edge he tucked his legs neatly under him
and soared into the air above the heads of the amazed audience. He circled twice before a security guard in the balcony had the presence of mind to open an upper-level exit
door. Out went Bill Grebec, birdman of Midway, gliding
gooney of justice, to join his compatriots.

24

Oh, Where? Oh, Where?

Now that there were thirty-five of them, I wondered where they hid themselves? How much time did they spend in their bodies, where did they stay, what did they eat? I received no more messages for a week and felt no inner impulses to jump on a jet to Peru or Texarkana or Mozambique.

Madly, desperately, I began to work again on my Fourteenth Street vaude extravaganza. I booked dancers, hired an orchestra, had playbills printed—all for a date I wasn't sure would ever arrive. But no contact came from the Thirty-Six to send me on my hunt for that final individual who would complete the set, fill the last piece in the puzzle, square the circle.

Meanwhile, the citizenry of Earth were devolving by subtle degrees. You may laugh, but it was registered in

little things—charity contributions dropped way down, for
instance. Domestic violence erupted into massacre with
frightening frequency. The shadowy game of cat and
mouse played out at sea by rival navies and in the sky by
opposing air forces became more deadly. Incidents of international tension became daily shrieking headlines.

Some few connected the world's decline with the appearance of the tent in Central Park and the preliminary
sounding of the shofar, but none grasped the whole truth.
How could they? That had been entrusted to me, Dexter
Sinister, ordinary, sinning, corrupt, neurotic Dexter. Why
me? The existential plea was a recurring theme in my head.
Why had I been selected? Okay, I had done a pretty good
job so far at hauling in their wayward members from the
ends of the earth; but the other half of the bargain, the
judgment, that's the part that concerned me now. That and
the one remaining Thirty-Sixer who apparently was eluding
the sensors of the others, for no word reached me, and my
opening loomed like an iceberg on the doomed horizon.

With the show less than a week away, I plunged into the
thousand tiny details that go into putting on a good show.

The city was ripe for a vaude revival. People wanted
anything that would remind them of the good old days. I
gave it to them.

The Fourteenth Street Theatre is a monument to the good
old days. Once a lavish vaude house, it had been reduced
in the past few years to a third-rate rock and wrestling
venue. The elaborately carved cornices at the corners of the
stage moldered under fifty years of dust; the stage curtains
were moth-eaten, the floorboards cracked and rotting; but
with a few buckets of paint and some soapy water, I was
able to put at least a superficial sheen on her—like a grand
old dame who peeks out at you from under a layer of mas-
cara and rouge.

The place was so old it still used canvas bags stuffed

with sand for counterweights, hand pulleys for ringing up the curtain, and big hot old Fresnels and troupers for lights. Most houses today have minispots on computerized grids —my guys had to climb out on catwalks to bend the barn doors by hand and slip the hand-cut gels into their frames —real old-fashioned methods, let me tell you.

The last band to play here set off fireworks onstage, burning a footwide circular gap in the boards. Or was that where Mad Dog Miller landed when Johnny the Jerk threw him out of the ring? Nobody could give me a straight story, but I had to patch more than one hole in the stage, and that doesn't even begin to detail the costs I rang up. Cleaning all the seats, for example, and steam-cleaning the house floor of fifty years of gum, tobacco, and candy residue, both cost a bundle.

Of course, I didn't pay for all this myself. I had angels, people who put up money for potential profit or more likely for a tax loss. I was supposed to be just the talent man, but no one else handled vaude shows, and I ended up producer by default.

I thought I'd do it up right for this show, since I didn't know when I might have the chance again, if ever. I phoned Lola and told her to wear something fabulous. I got out the tux and top hat, and rented a limo for myself and for several of the aging vaude stars in the revue. I got a couple of those hokey searchlights-on-wheels to crisscross the sky with some fake excitement and enticed the local New York TV stations to give me some coverage, Hollywood-style, of the old heroes of vaudeville making their curbside entrances. It's amazing what you can do with a few yards of red carpet and some klieg lights.

I don't want to brag, but it was quite a "galaxy of stars" that gathered under the eye-popping marquee that night. The mayor came, trying to hog the publicity as usual, but the onlookers were more interested in seeing the last surviving member of the Three Stooges than His Honor.

Of course, all the greats were gone. Kate Smith, Eddie Foy, W.C. Fields, the Marx boys, Bert Williams, the great dance teams, all were long dead. In fact, the representation of true vaude stars was thin. What we had were a lot of second-generation vaude people, lesser or faded B-movie stars really, whose parents had been the true article. It was just too long ago, now, for the real thing, but still the evening had a nice feel to it as limo after limo pulled up to cheers from the geriatric groupies who made up the crowd.

Lola got her picture on page 2 of the *Daily News* for the flash of flesh she gave the photog as she bent to exit the white Bentley. The vivid color of her eyes and the stunning black luster of her hair lost something in the change to grainy black and white, but the décolletage translated well.

This time I'd smartened up and given the MC duties to an old pro, a cigar-smoking wisecracker who'd outlived all his performing brothers and sisters and wives and lovers and friends and was really the last true representative of the dying art. I was able to sit down in row 3 center and enjoy the show.

I'm not going to give you a blow-by-blow of the show —you had to be there. Any description of the array of talent assembled on that one night would fall short of capturing the dizzying sense of a piece of history restored, for one glorious night, to life and action. Cakewalkers cakewalked, stride pianists strode, knockabout comics knocked about, all the old and varied arts resurfaced for a few hours on a stage on East Fourteenth Street, like time-travelers in a bubbly capsule, dancing and singing away in our special corner of the universe.

The night would have been perfect for me, if my pernicious bookkeeper hadn't pointed out to me an anomaly in the ticket sales. A block of thirty-five seats had been paid for and picked up "by a young boy in a psychedelic paisley yarmulke," the bookkeeper remembered. No one sat in those seats that night, at least no one visible. Yet as I watched, I knew that my humble show was being judged on a scale I had not intended.

25

White Dwarf, Brown Dwarf, and Red Giants

After the Fourteenth Street Show, I took a weekend off with Lola. I was burned out on show business and on chasing the Thirty-Six. Only one remained to be found; but right at the moment, I couldn't marshal my energies to head out to Midway, Alaska, or parts unknown.

Lola and I drove out to the cozy Amagansett cottage from whose skies Mr. Chin had approached me in the form of a Canadian goose. This time I hoped only for peace and quiet and a few hours with Lola.

Of course, she wanted to hit the bars in Southampton, East Hampton, Sag Harbor, Amagansett, and Montauk. A few years ago, I would have enjoyed it more. Now that I was settling comfortably into middle-age, noisy bars and rock bands no longer had the smoky allure they once had. I tagged along obediently; after all, this was her weekend, too. We toured some of the fashionable watering holes of the Hamptons, ending up at Sam's on Main Street in East Hampton—not that fashionable but friendly, more my kind of place, almost a New York City bar, if you know what I mean.

The warm, boozy atmosphere at the bar was broken by a collection of landlubbing would-be yacht captains in white pants, blue blazers, and soft leather boat shoes, the new old guard of the Hamptons (real money drinks at home), hobnobbing and hassling the pretty young waitresses, many of whom were actresses fleeing New York for the summer. Lola and I took a booth in the back and ordered up a pitcher of margaritas.

When we'd settled in, Lola stared at me from across the table and said, "Dexter, I'm worried about you."

"Oh, I'm all right," I answered. "Nothing a weekend in the Hamptons won't cure."

"No, I mean it, you're pushing yourself too hard."

"Look who's talking." My criticism of her as the driven young advertising capitalist was part of our standard dialogue, those pat, rehearsed lines couples spew out when they don't want to talk about what's really bothering them. She was the driven capitalist; I was the dreamer.

"Have you thought about seeing a psychiatrist?" she continued.

Page 2 of our script. She was continuously in therapy, for which I saw no reason, and I refused to go even to a preliminary interview. I hold to the theorem of the poet Ezra Pound, who said, roughly: "Kill my devils and you'll kill my angels, too."

"No." I was feeling a little hostile, but the sour-sweet margaritas took the edge off. "Honest, Lola, I'm fine. I just put on a good show, brought in some big receipts, you got your picture in the paper, glamorous, what could be better?"

"You talked in your sleep last night." It sounded like an accusation.

"A woman's name?" I asked lightly.

"I wish. That would have been easy to take."

"What, then?"

"You mumbled something about 'Jewish cowboys,' whatever that means."

"I don't remember a thing." When I was really tired, I often fell into a deep sleep from which I recalled no dreams.

"Yes, and then—" Lola looked around as if an embarrassing revelation was to follow, "then you started flapping your wings like you wanted to take off. I hope you're going to be okay," she said.

"Thanks," I answered, sincerely grateful that someone cared enough about me to voice concern. I wondered myself about the "Jewish cowboys" bit. The flying part was self-explanatory. Obviously, I wished to join the Thirty-Six, become like them, fly in the heavens like them, among pillars of clouds, which, if I failed in my mission, would soon become pillars of fire.

"So, what are you going to about it?" Lola asked.

"What?"

"The talking in the sleep, the flying dreams."

"Oh, they'll pass, Lola. Just as soon as I find the last of them—"

"Oh, Dexter."

"What?"

"You're not still going on about that, are you?"

"I am."

Lola looked even more worried than before. "But, Dex, they're gone. They might never have been here. I'm beginning to think you made the whole thing up about knowing them—"

That was my fault. I hadn't told her about all my travels

since the disappearance of the tent, and explaining was difficult. I had to prove to her that I wasn't crazy.

"Let me tell you a story called 'White Dwarf, Brown Dwarf, and Red Giants,' related to me by a thirteen-year-old boy named Joshua Levy, who is one of the Thirty-Six. As you hear this, I hope you'll understand that I never could have made it up by myself, that it had to come from the mouth of one far wiser than me."

The idea of my telling her a story appealed to Lola. She undoubtedly thought it would be good therapy for me, as she enjoyed playing amateur psychiatrist. So, we both got what we wanted.

"Once there were two red giants, named Fearsome and Awesome, who lived in the sky. They were fiery spirits. If anyone approached them, they rumbled and belched and spewed and thundered.

"'I'm Fearsome—' the one red giant would boil and burn.

"'I'm Awesome—' his brother would flare and glare.

"That was usually enough to scare anyone away; but one day they were visited by a pair of wandering dwarf fire spirits, a brown dwarf and a white dwarf, spinning around each other."

"Dexter—" Lola tried to interrupt.

But I pushed on. "Fearsome and Awesome were mighty upset that these two dwarfs would pass through their domain without so much as a 'How do you do?'

"'Let's bake them,' said Awesome.

"'Let's roast them,' said Fearsome."

"Dexter—" Lola interjected, but I was lost deep in memory and didn't hear her.

"But the dwarfs, though they glowed less brightly, were denser; and the red giants, though huge, were old and tired and losing their heat. The dwarfs spun and danced and so disoriented the two red giants that they fell apart and then exploded, and that was the end of Fearsome and Awesome. The moral of the story is the same as that of David and Goliath: 'Giants don't always win.'"

"Dexter—"

"A young boy told me that story. Don't you see? How could he know about such things unless he had been out there, among the stars?"

Lola took my hand and led me from the bar. Only then did I realize that nearly everyone in the place had listened. The magic of the tale had drawn them in, even when narrated by an inferior storyteller like me. They applauded as we left, further embarrassing Lola and pleasing me.

"That was a wonderful story, Dex, but it doesn't prove anything."

"I suppose not."

"But I love you anyway, you foolish starry-eyed dreamer."

"And I love you, Lola," I answered. My mind drifted back to the bar, and the strange spell that had come over me.

Maybe I've been too hard on Lola Corolla. Yes, she's beautiful, and years younger than me, but I shouldn't hold those attributes against her. Perhaps the disparity in our ages explains the vast differences in the way we view the world. When I was growing up, we questioned everything. Her generation went for the bucks. Some people just don't understand the mysterious. Does that statement make any sense? Can anyone comprehend the ineffable? Anyway, Lola's one of those who believes in objective reality. That's not a criticism. We can't all be alike. Some people, honest realists such as Lola, cannot see the veiling shadow of mystery; they see only the hard concrete wall of life. Are they penetrating illusion or missing something? I don't know.

26

Jewish Gauchos
of the Pampas

Long ago, in a musty corner of my hometown public library, on a back shelf among the dull, mostly unread histories, I found a book called *Jewish Gauchos of the Pampas*, by Alberto Gerchunoff. He had compiled a fascinating, little-known history of the Jewish emigration to South America.

On the grassy plains of Argentina are vast tracts of grazing land much like the American Southwest. The legendary gaucho, the South American cowboy, is renowned for his riding and roping, just as is his West Texas counterpart. But what is not widely known is that among these Argentine ranchers are Jews, refugees from pogroms in Eastern Europe, who have adapted to the wild ways of the range and are now successful cattlemen and members of their country's elite landed gentry.

The dim memory of this book worked its way up through my consciousness until it suggested itself as a place to look for the last Thirty-Sixer. It wasn't divine inspiration as with my trips to Nome and Nuku'alofa, but it was all I had to go on, since my contact with the thirty-five was nil.

The Fourteenth Street show had been a total sellout. The coffers of the Dexter Sinister Variety Arts Talent Agency were bursting with dineros. I could afford a quick Buenos Aires vacation, and if I found what I sought, so much the better. I booked a flight for the next morning.

The pampas are more like the plains of eastern Colorado or the California inland valleys than Texas: flat, grassy, ideal grazing land for sheep or cattle. I don't know what I expected, but what I saw from the train car that brought me to Escuria in the dusty Argentine plains were Spanish cowboys, not at all Jewish-looking, differing from North American cowboys only in the amount of spangly silver their horses wore for decoration and by the crisp flat round cut of their hats. As did Texas cowpokes, gauchos used pickup trucks, helicopters, and small planes as much as horses for ranchwork these days.

Since I had no connections this trip, I'd arbitrarily picked a town from a railroad schedule once I got to Buenos Aires. My Spanish, spiced with a crude Puerto Rican salsa flavor from living in New York, nearly deserted me. When the train conductor called the name of the town, I'd almost forgotten which one it was and had to jump out in a hurry as the train began to lurch away from the station. It wouldn't have mattered if I'd gotten off a stop ahead or two stops early, I suppose, since I was working by synchronicity again, letting the random element be the determining factor. What else did I have to go on?

The train station, though small, was reassuringly similar to train stations the world over, replete with wooden benches and a large clock, its rails a comforting link to the rest of life.

I walked through the station and out the other side onto the streets of Escuria, feeling like a character in a Jorge Luis Borges novel, who is about to meet himself from the past, or enter a fictitious library full of strangely titled books that have never been written, or die in a knife fight for no reason. The dry heat of the plains made everything seem plastic and fantastical. I looked for a bar.

That was easy. Escuria seemed to be all bars. The train station was in the worst part of town, as are most train stations. The bars of Escuria had no doors on them, and the action spilled onto the street from in front of several, as men hung out at the doorway, clear bottles of golden-colored beer in their hands.

My brother once told me, "Don't go into any bars without windows." This is a sensible piece of advice for numerous reasons—windows give you a second escape route if you need one in case of fire or riot. Also, any place without windows could be trying to hide what goes on inside. Well, not one of the bars in Escuria had windows.

But I was thirsty. I had to disregard Joe's advice. Suitcase in hand, I picked the friendliest-looking spot I could find, a little joint called El Bolo. Nobody hung out in front of El Bolo, but I didn't know if this boded well or evil for me. I stepped inside.

Bars, like train stations, have a certain universal sameness. For instance, it was smoky inside, as was almost every bar I'd ever been to except a few flaky places in California. Also, it was dim. Did I say dim? Let me go all out and say dark. What little light there was came from the narrow doorless opening. It was as murky as late twilight, but it was also twenty degrees cooler just inside the doorway.

Once my eyes adjusted to the lack of light, I saw a few

tables, mostly unoccupied, and a counter at the rear. There was no bar per se; the room was really more a cafe. I crossed confidently to the counter. A middle-aged Argentine in a white shirt and black pants leaned against a sink behind him and looked at me. The work table next to the sink was littered with dirty glasses and small tapa plates. The bartender didn't seem to be in a big hurry to wash the dishes or wait on me, as he smoked a hand-rolled cigarette, cupping it in one hand against the wind even though we were indoors. *Retired cowboy,* I thought.

"Uno cerveza, por favor," I said.

The Argentine blinked and crinkled his eyes. Lines of laughter spread across his leathery face, but he only said quietly: "Señor, I think we do better to speak English."

I appreciated that. He could have made fun of me, but he didn't.

"My name is Dexter Sinister."

"Ramon Fuentes."

We shook hands. He offered me a cotton bag of tobacco. I declined. Ramon opened a freezer beneath the counter and pulled a bottle of beer from a tub of water with ice cubes floating in it. The freezer came equipped with a built-in bottle opener, which Ramon used. I calculated the freezer to be a thirties model, worth plenty on the U.S. collectibles market.

"Thank you."

Ramon nodded.

"I'm looking for—" but that was as far as I got.

"I know what the señor is looking for."

"You do?"

"Yes. Like most men, he is looking for a woman."

"No, that's not it."

Ramon was unfazed. He didn't get excited when I told him he was wrong. He was probably right, at some level. "What, then?" he asked.

I figured, what the hell? It might as well be a dishwashing cowboy in a rundown village cafe as anybody else. "There any Jewish gauchos in this part of the pampas?" I asked.

"Si, Señor. I myself am Jewish. Most of the town is Jewish."

"You don't wear yarmulkes?"

"Only on Sabbath."

"Do you know the legend of the Thirty-Six Just Men?" —my litmus question.

"Yes—oh, but you—the señor,"—Ramon began to laugh—"does not think—oh, no!" The Argentine collapsed in high-pitched laughter. "Not me, ha ha ha!"

"You're not—" I tried to confirm, but this sent him into fresh peals of hilarity. Obviously, I had made a gross error.

When Ramon finally recovered himself, he poured thick ruby-red local wine into a plain drinking glass and raised it to me.

"The señor has come a long way for nothing. This is a village of sinners. No trace of holiness is to be found here. When the shofar next blows, for us it will be Judgment Day. Do you understand?" Ramon tilted his head back and drank deeply.

Suddenly he was no longer laughing but somber. "We heard the ram's horn sound here, while everyone else read about it in the paper or saw it on the television. It blew as clearly here as in New York. Do you grasp what I am saying to you? That is why men crowd the cafes. This used to be a busy, prosperous town. Now the whole population merely drinks and waits mindlessly for the end.

"But come, señor, I will show you."

It was siesta time. Ramon closed up the bar and brought me around to the alley behind the main street. A wooden shed sagged against the back of the building for support. As Ramon fiddled with its door latch, I worried for a mo-

ment that he was going to bring out and saddle up horses
and ask me to ride with him, an absurd impossibility, but
instead he revealed his pride and joy, a monstrous 1962
DeSoto that took up every inch of the weary shack. Before
I could get in, I had to wait until he squeezed himself into
the oversized vehicle and maneuvered his way out of the
lean-to and into the alley.

We drove out of town, into a waving sea of pampas
grass. Even the DeSoto, so aptly named for this oceanic
billowing land we traversed, was dwarfed by the immensity of the plain. I had seen it from the train, of course, but
here in a single automobile I felt even more its rolling,
marine majesty.

"The pampa region is not a true plain but a gently sloping set of uninterrupted low hills, what your Kansas must
have been a hundred years ago," Ramon informed me as
we steered along a dirt road bordered on one side by grass
taller than a man, sloping on the other down to a flat,
shiny, slow-moving stream in a broader expanse of plain.
The sight of the horsemen of the pampas steering recalci-
trant cattle across a wash brought back memories of a
hundred childhood television westerns.

"We had an artist in town, a man of great vision, a true
Argentine renaissance man. He liked to do things big—
two years ago he planted a twenty-acre field of light and
dark crops in patterns that blossomed into a replica of Da
Vinci's *Mona Lisa*, visible only from the air. It only lasted
a few weeks, but it was magnificent.

"Last year he set to work with bulldozers and carved a
pampas horseman out of a small hill. I could have taken
you to see that one, but I wanted you to see instead how his
spirit was moved by the blowing of the horn of doom."

The dirt road gave out and we crossed open plain,
Ramon wheeling the DeSoto over virgin ground as if it
were a four-wheeled jeep. After a while we were so far out

into the vastness I couldn't even tell where we were in relation to Escuria. Only train tracks off in the distance and parallel telephone wires running beside them gave any hint of direction, as overhead the sun slept through siesta without casting a shadow on the featureless landscape.

Then, off in the distance, I saw them. They looked like totem poles. At once, I knew how many without even counting them—arranged in remote grandeur in a Stonehenge-like circle. Black, monolithic, they contrasted vividly against the swaying wheat-colored pampas. We were still miles from them.

"They must be immense," I said in awe. "How did the artist build them? How did he lever them into place?"

"He swore he did not, señor."

"Huh?"

"The artist claimed that he only conceived the idea. That it built itself."

"How do you mean?"

"He said he had a dream of this arrangement and came out here the next day to find it already up. He offered as proof the fact that there was no evidence of construction, no bulldozer, steam shovel, or backhoe tracks, no trails from diggings. In fact, if you look, the base of each pole is not set in concrete but driven straight into the ground as if driven by a huge pile driver or—" Ramon paused dramatically.

"Yes?"

"Or hurled into the earth from the firmament, as the artist believed."

We approached the poles, their magnificent desolation and austere placement not diminished by nearness. A hundred yards away, Ramon stopped the DeSoto and turned to me.

"And now, señor, you must go on alone."

"Why?" I asked, surprised. "You'll wait for me here, won't you?"

"I will wait, but the señor must enter the circle of poles alone, as decreed in the artist's dream."

"I was in the artist's dream? Where is he? I want to talk to him."

Ramon regarded me sadly. "I am sorry, señor. Three days after the dream, he died. His last words were that a stranger would come to town, and that he should stand in the center of the circle."

"What for?"

"He did not say, and alas, we cannot ask him. We have been waiting for you ever since. Now, will the señor please go?"

I went. I crossed the length of a football field on shaky legs and paused when I reached the outermost circle, for it turned out that the thirty-six poles were arranged in three concentric circles of twelve, offset so as to appear an un- broken circle from a distance. I estimated the height of the poles to be at least sixty feet, or roughly double the height of your average telephone pole, and thrice the girth. They were black-lacquered like Japanese wood, smooth and shiny and formidable. I entered the circles and passed through the middle one and into the inner one and finally came to the smallish clearing at the center of the formation.

There was nothing but a matted-down area of pampas grass, as if deer or cattle had slept there. Instinctively, I moved to the very center and looked out at the carefully placed arrangement of giant logs, a spiky ebony symbolic rendering of the object of my search. What could its mean- ing be? Why had an Argentine artist dreamed it and the Thirty-Six erected it? There could be no doubt that this was their handiwork. Why had they lured me all the way to Argentina to see it?

The wind, finding an obstruction in its unfettered sweep

across the plains, whistled irritatingly as it hurried through the ring. I sat down and patiently waited, expecting a visitation, but received only wind-blown dust and silence. At last, restless, I stood up. Just then the wind picked up, and the upright logs of the ring began to vibrate and resonate like ethereal wind chimes. I sat down again. The ringing, echoing sound intensified and then I heard a single word, coalescing in clarity out of the wind-driven ringing of the poles:

"Soon!" it said.

I jumped up and back. "Who said that?" I yelled. Never had the divine intervened so close by. I peeked around several of the poles foolishly, but I was alone. I could see Ramon in the DeSoto a hundred yards away. I waited a long, long time for further words, but none came. When I returned to the car and told Ramon what had happened, he said nothing, nodding sadly as if it confirmed his worst fears. We drove in silence back toward Escuria.

There was a purpose to what had happened here, and I knew what it was. I was meant to receive this message. It was intended to spur me on, like a prophet's lament: "Turn back, O men of God." There was no Thirty-Sixth Just Man in Escuria. Instead was a small corner of the earth already frozen in fear of the imminent judgment, and a dying artist's depiction of that judgment to come, a living sculpture that spoke to me alone. Ramon dropped me at the train station in Escuria, and I caught the next express back to Buenos Aires.

27

Visitation

I'd been cast adrift at sea, I'd had fifty pounds of explosives nearly go off in my face, I'd been sent on merry chases to the ends of the earth, for what? Vaguely I understood that, like Job, I was being tested while I toiled. What grades I received, I do not know. After my fruitless trip to Escuria, I determined to wait for some definite signal before embarking on any more human scavenger hunts.

I lolled around the office, not willing to take on any more big projects such as the revival show, but not willing either to make any effort on my own to find the last Thirty-Sixer. I needed direction.

I remembered that while the tent was up, during the time of the blowing of the ram's horn, a group of believers in the Thirty-Six had sprung up. I heard that in California it had become big business, with seminars and health-spa weekends devoted to it—a whole thriving New Age Thirty-Six industry. Naturally, there were a few local Manhattan chapters.

The upper West Side had its own unit, meetings scheduled every Monday night at seven o'clock at the West Side YMHA. After closing up my office one Monday, I headed uptown and visited one of the Cuban-Chinese places on upper Broadway that offer *Comidas Chinas et Criollas*. I chowed down on some chow mein and black beans, bucked up with a couple of cups of wickedly strong Cafe Bustelo, and was ready for a heady meeting with a group of people who could not know what I knew, that their wildest flights of imagination were exceeded by the bizarre reality of the Thirty-Six.

Imagine my surprise, then, on entering the conference room at the Y and finding Joshua Levy lecturing earnestly to the crowd. There must have been fifty or sixty people in the room. I recognized none of them. I did note that they were all nearing middle-age, mostly Jewish-looking (not unusual for the upper West Side or for the YMHA), and that they all looked at Joshua with reverence as a guru, which indeed he was.

I was reminded again of a young Jesus, but this time it seemed more like the scene after the Resurrection when Jesus appeared before the apostles, "the doors being shut," as it says in John 20:26, a neat magic trick, and "stood in their midst," and Thomas thrust a hand in His side.

Joshua glanced up when I entered the room and smiled shyly toward me, then continued his talk.

"So we see that the old ways are coming to an end. Families no longer live together, men no longer farm or hunt together, all the ties that bind are being loosed. The result is degeneration of the moral fiber. To right things, we must somehow restitch the moral fabric, sew the rips, snip off the trailing loose ends.

"This may be a painful process, as treating a wound can be. It may kill us, as surgery sometimes does. But not to attempt it is to watch the cancer spread without trying any therapy, to let it rot us away from within without attempting corrective measures. And we cannot wait for someone else to do it. The attempt must start with the people in this room."

Wise beyond his years, the young boy lectured these jaded upper West Siders on their moral inferiority. The attitude in the room was one of chastened guilt and rectifying fervor, as one finds at a sales meeting.

As Josh sent them away, full of messianic visions and evangelistic energy, I hung around to talk to him, waiting while he spoke a few extra words to extremely devoted disciples. I also wanted to see how he'd make his exit, whether he'd jump from the window ledge or simply disappear, or what.

When they had all gone, Joshua turned to me: "Well, Dexter, where is our lonely last man?"

"I don't know. Isn't it a bit late for this?" I gestured to the recently emptied room of believers.

"Oh, you never know. There could be a turning, and it could start with any one of these people, who knows? Don't misinterpret us, Dexter. We're not omnipotent. If we were, there would be no need for the meeting, and no need for your valuable assistance. But we cannot hold out much longer. You must search harder for him."

"Was Jesus one of the Just Men of his age?" I asked quickly, not even sure myself why the question suddenly popped into my head.

"The justest. The host with the mostest!" Joshua said playfully. "Now, I must go."

This was the moment I had waited for. "Where do you stay these days, Josh? The whole gang, I mean." Josh lifted the yarmulke off his head and scratched his short curls.

"We've taken up residence in the torch at the Statue of Liberty. Kind of symbolic, don't you think?"

"Don't the federal park rangers chase you out?" I wondered aloud.

"Oh, we're not inside the torch. There's some fine pigeon nesting spots out on the points of the flame. The whole group is up there."

"I see," I said, envisioning the Thirty-Six as a gritty flock of urban birds. "So, are you going to wing it over there now?" I asked.

"Naw," he said. "I'll catch the tourist ferry in the morning. Tonight I preach all night. There are other meetings, some in fancy apartments, some underneath Grand Central Station in the dens of the homeless. I'm trying to reach everyone I can with the message, before we convene."

"And when is that?" I asked, fearing the answer.

"When you finish your work," Joshua admonished me.

"Don't you have any hints? I mean, if you can't find him with your combined power, how can I?"

"We're not detectives, Dexter. You are, of a sort anyhow. Make the fullest use of your talents. Somewhere on this earth a man or woman waits for you. Perhaps he or she is incapacitated and can't reach out to us. Perhaps it is someone incarcerated, or forbidden to leave a restricted area, for whatever reasons. Perhaps it is one who cannot hear or speak, yet who longs to be with us."

"So many possibilities." My head spun just thinking about it. "I'll try harder," I said, though I had no idea what to do.

"That is all we ask."

Overwhelmed by the difficulty of it all, I slumped into a chair to think, and I didn't even notice when Joshua disappeared, either by magic or by ordinary means.

28

Corolla's Corona

The next morning I called my erstwhile girlfriend, Lola
Corolla. "I bet you're one of those blasé New Yorkers
who's never been to the Statue of Liberty," I said.

"Wrong, smartass. My whole PS 105 sixth-grade class
went there on a field trip. We also did the Empire State
Building. Next question?"

"How 'bout taking a ride with me out to see the old lady.
They've dolled her up since PS 105 went."

"What's this all about, Dexter?"

"I just want to take a nice romantic ferry ride," I lied.

"Well, I have worked the last six Saturdays. I suppose I
could take the afternoon off."

"Great."

We stood in line with tourists from all the states and
many nations, then crowded aboard the ferry. It was hardly

the stuff of romance. Lola can't go inside on these rides or she gets seasick; so we stood on the bow, on this sparkling September afternoon, six weeks after the blowing of the shofar.

For some reason known only to navigational pilots, the ferry makes a wide swing, looping past lower Manhattan before arcing out toward the statue. A strong sea breeze had blown the haze of pollution away on this early fall day, and the buildings of the city jumped out in sharp relief one behind the other, making the place seem airy and magical and clean. A grand illusion. I put my arm around Lola, and we goggled at the cityscape.

Soon the statue swung into view on the port side. We moved as a group from the ferry to the entrance at the massive concrete base, where the National Park Service Center and Gift Shop were located. Her scale, somewhat diminished by the size of New York harbor and the distance from shore, was impressive up close. Craning my neck, I looked toward the upraised arm with its monumental torch but saw no flutter of wings.

"Come on, let's walk up. It'll be good aerobics," Lola suggested.

I groaned but agreed reluctantly.

Three hundred and thirty-five steps later, we reached the five-pointed crown, which was as high as you could climb in the statue. Lola was in terrific shape. I was ready to call for the paramedics.

The guide was a young woman in her late twenties who obviously had given the speech a few hundred times too many. On and on she droned, her back to the marvelous view of the harbor. How could she, or Lola, or any of the gathered tourists know what true wonders ringed the head of the "mighty woman with a torch," as Emma Lazarus called her?

I surreptitiously tried the door to the arm that holds the

torch, but it was locked. Yes, the Thirty-Sixers'd picked a nice secure roost for themselves.

Defeated in my effort to reach them and talk to them, I coerced Lola into taking the elevator down. As we were herded along with the rest of the group back toward the ferry, I stepped out from the flow of the crowd to look back up at the distant torch one last time. Yes! There they were, a flash of wings in the sunlight, a swooping dive and turn all in unison.

"Lola," I said, pointing, "look at that."

"Yeah, what a shame. They ought to poison them all, or shoot them. Imagine all those pigeons crapping on Miss Liberty."

"No, Lola, honey, you don't understand. Those are them. You know, the ones from the tent, the ones I tried to introduce you to."

"Have you lost it altogether, Dexter?" She looked at me worriedly. Just then the thirty-five buzzed us, circling in the missing-man formation, dipping their wings in salute to me, their white underfeathers like a corona around the sun-lit black of my Lola's beautiful hair. Her eyes wide with fear, Lola clutched at my arm as we hurried for the boat.

29

New Age
Old-Time Religion

From Elvis Presley Plaza in Memphis, Tennessee, to Wayne Newton Boulevard in Las Vegas, Nevada, yea and verily even unto Frank Sinatra Drive in Palm Springs, California, the people of our nation and the world began to express their yearning. It became a great national religious revival, initiated no doubt by the undeniably miraculous though ephemeral appearance of the tent in Central Park.

The cult of the Thirty-Six flourished, as one might imagine, but so did any group promoting apocalyptic notions, and that included the vast and powerful network of television evangelists, most of them Baptists, Assembly of God preachers of the divine infallibility of the Bible.

Just how they fit the episode of the tent into their arcane visions I was not sure, but I had heard them work greater miracles. The coming of the Thirty-Six, with its built-in Judeo-Christian symbology, was made to order for the ministries of the airwaves.

One of the biggest of the big was Aaron Bateman of the Church of Divine Retribution in Corpus Christi, Texas. When he rented the Felt Forum in Madison Square Garden and promised to deliver a fire-breathing testimony on his personal meetings with the Thirty-Six, I thought I better check out the action.

Bateman offered a healing portion of his service—and the power of his personality was enough to send most devotees into rapture at his touch. Those who weren't immediately bowled over backward into the waiting arms of his assistants were given a special blessing not unlike the Vulcan pressure hold; he pinched their carotid artery, rendering them temporarily senseless.

But the healing schtick was just the preliminary—the warmup act in this arena where I'd witnessed so many boxing matches and music concerts. Everyone awaited the boiling, gushing geyser of energy when Aaron Bateman let loose with one of his fiery sermons. I was probably the only unbeliever in an audience of three thousand, unless you count the bored concessionaires and the house security. I hung back by the exits. I wanted to be able to escape onto Eighth Avenue in a hurry if I needed to.

You could not convince me that the Thirty-Six would have anything to do with Aaron Bateman. It was too implausible. He couldn't be number Thirty-Six. Remember, this was my hobby. Long ago I'd collected information on Bateman—beginning with tax evasion and continuing through philandering and pederasty to right-wing conspiracies for the violent overthrow of the country. From my point of view, the man was an out-and-out psycho. To his adoring followers, he was the nearest thing to a representative of the Almighty on earth, much closer to Him than the unholy pope, who was practically a Communist in the minds of Bateman's believers.

As a speaker Bateman was a tub-thumping, old-style roarer, who sometimes modulated to a whisper, playing with the subtle qualities of amplified speech, using expensive microphones and PA equipment backed by a flashy ten-piece band.

He slithered roundabout into the subject of the Thirty-Six. You could see he was still formulating his ideas on this matter, because like most people he didn't know yet whether the whole episode was over.

"Brethren," he shouted, then leaned over the Bible he held in front of him like a talisman, "hear the Holy Scripture—from the Book of Revelation—"

Of course he's using Revelation, I thought, *the great mysterious text that can mean anything to anyone!*

"Revelation, chapter twenty, verses twelve to fifteen: 'And I saw the dead, small and great, stand before God; and the books were opened: and another book was opened, which is the book of life: and the dead were judged out of those things which were written in the books, according to their works. And the sea gave up the dead which were in it; and death and hell delivered up the dead which were in them.' Picture it, folks. All the dead come back to life, but only to be judged. 'And they were judged every man according to their works. And death and hell were cast into the lake of fire. This is the second death. And whosoever was not found written in the book of life was cast into the lake of fire.'"

Bateman paused dramatically. You could have heard a pin drop with untold numbers of angels on its head. "Pretty important to get your name in that book, isn't it, my friends?" So far he hadn't said one thing I would argue with, but he hadn't yet tied in to the Thirty-Six. It was coming.

"Two months ago in Central Park, my brethren, a tent appeared, a nomadic arab's tent—think about it, friends, a biblical tent. The civil and military authorities were powerless to remove it, nor could they cross an invisible line into it.

"Yet some few among us were able to enter. Who were these people? The rumor spread that they were emissaries from God. As your pastor, I could do no less than come to New York myself—this den of iniquity you true believers somehow manage to inhabit, and God blesses you for it— come to this evil city and confront these strangers myself.

"And I am here to tell you today that the Thirty-Six are real, glory be to God! The judgment is at hand!" There was a stirring in the audience. The principle on which Aaron Bateman's ministry, and all such others, is based is repentance. The apocalypse must always be imminent but should never arrive—just as in the theory of limits—for if it actually comes, then it is too late.

"I tell you, friends, the hour is upon us. In the dead of night, they took me into their tent—"

I listened closely, incredulous, as he described his meeting with the Thirty-Six. He mentioned, among others, a young boy, an Asian man, three elderly ladies, an old Eskimo woman, a Tongan chieftain. There could be no doubt; he had met the Thirty-Six. I saw that they worked in mysterious ways, their wonders to perform.

"They ordered me, your preacher, to repent, and they sent me back into the world with that message for all. And so I am here to tell you tonight those things for which I must publicly unburden myself."

And there before this crowd, Bateman began to recount his life of debauchery, venality, and greed. His audience, his devoted flock, in shock and disbelief, walked out, for this was not the message they had come to hear.

Soon Bateman was speaking to only a few score hard-core believers. He dropped the microphone and sat down on the edge of the stage to continue his monumental confession, a litany of sins that would take him until dawn of the next day to complete.

30

His Shining Appearance

A person is, after all, only a human being,
and sometimes not even that.
—Shirley Kumove *Words Like Arrows*

As the world teeter-tottered on the brink of self-destruc-
tion, the Thirty-Six demonstrated for me their immense
power to effect *tikkun,* that transformative healing we all so
desperately needed. I was out walking in the park late one
afternoon, wistfully, forlornly hoping for a repeat performance of the tent show, when three of the Thirty-Sixers
manifested themselves before me.

It was an unlikely triumvirate: Bill Grebec, the ungainly
gooney; Miss Betty, my Eskimo find; and Andrew Scoggins, the Maine potato farmer. Frankly, they resembled a
trio of runaways from a Bowery mission more than the

saviors of the world. I wondered aloud at their shabby appearance and received a lecture from severe but correct farmer Scoggins.

"You must remembah, Sinistah," he scolded in his flat Maine accents, "we do not curry favor from any man. Our mandate comes from above. Only we who have glimpsed His shining appearance can face the realities of this world. Clothes have nothing to do with it."

"You mean, like the face of God?" I asked naively.

Bill Grebec answered, gawking at me and turning his head from side to side like a parrot to sight on me better. "Call it what you will. The Hebrew term is *Shekhina*, the 'Divine Presence.' From Him all blessings flow. We are only His intermediaries. But enough, we have a job to do today—"

"You mean, you're on a mission from God?" I offered, but the three Thirty-Sixers chose to ignore me.

"Come with us," Miss Betty said firmly. I wondered where we were going. I knew of no nearby wars, famines, or disasters where we might intervene immediately, unless you were among the cynics who counted the whole metropolitan area as one big disaster area.

They had rousted a van from somewhere to transport us. On its side someone had painted a company name and slogan: HEAVENLY LAUNDRY—DEEP CLEANING.

I believed it.

"Where are we headed?" I asked as Bill Grebec opened the sliding door of the van and motioned for me to enter.

"A trouble spot," he answered enigmatically.

I could never look at him without thinking of that magical moment when he rose from the stage at the birdwatchers' convention. The thought of him driving an ordinary panel truck seemed somehow amusing.

Miss Betty took the passenger's seat; Mr. Scoggins and I

sat on piles of clean towels in the back of the truck. I wondered if they had hijacked the thing, stolen it, or made friends among the natives.

There were no windows on the sides or back of the truck, but an occasional glimpse out the front told me where we were going. We worked our way downtown through the beginnings of a crunching New York rush hour, finally pouring out of the Holland Tunnel just ahead of the masses of New Jersey commuters. We took the Jersey Turnpike south down to the massive refinery at Port Elizabeth, which I had only seen as a network of glowing lights at night and smelled by day as a foul stench blowing across a stark landscape of girders, pipes, and oil tanks.

We parked outside a fence along a service road to the refinery and waited for dark. I had no idea what we were doing there, but I expected Miss Betty to stay in the van. But when the time came, she hopped down spritely and we all stood before the eight-foot fence, a thick mesh topped by coils of rolled barb wire.

"What's up, Bill?" I asked.

"Trouble inside."

"How do you know?" I asked, but withdrew the question at once. How did they know anything? How did Bill Grebec fly? How did they find me?

I was hoping they'd burn a hole in the fence with their eyes or some other spectacular manifestation, but instead Andrew Scoggins took an ordinary pair of wire clippers from his overalls pocket and proceeded to clip open a hole large enough for each of us to wedge through.

Soon we were walking among the steaming exhaust vents, plumy burnoff flames, and twinkling lights of the refinery plant. It was a futuristic setting, eerily lit by harsh yellow carbon-arc worklights. We hid from occasional forklift traffic, but the whole area was strangely underpopulated, as if it ran itself.

"What is our objective?" I asked, but Bill Grebec only motioned for us to follow him, until we huddled in the shadow of an immense tank, brimming with God knew what volatile fuel.

"If one of these babies blows, it'll break windows on Wall Street," I commented to no one in particular. Standing next to all that liquid petroleum was no more dangerous than driving into a gas station and parking over six thousand gallons of it—in either circumstance an explosion would be fatal. But somehow when you're right next to these reservoirs full of the stuff, it seems more threatening.

"This one is going to explode if we don't do something about it," Bill informed me.

"How do you—" I started to ask, then switched tacks. "But, I mean, they monitor these things, there are inspections, safeguards, redundant backup systems—"

"Nonetheless, this one will ignite in . . . how long, Miss Betty?"

"Twenty-three minutes."

" . . . Twenty-three minutes, if we don't intercede."

"But how? Why?"

"Oh, the usual thing—a combination of poor workmanship on the original welds, faulty construction—the thing was put together half a foot to the east of where the plans called for. Then tonight a certain safety valve stuck open, and the watchman on this shift was late leaving a whorehouse in Newark. He's half an hour late on his rounds; but it's midnight and who's going to know, he thinks, especially since he long ago figured out how to dummy the times on the key-clock device he punches on his rounds. Tonight it would have cost him and a few thousand other people their lives—"

"Hey, now wait a second, Bill. These refinery fires are spectacular, but they don't usually harm anyone outside of plant workers and firemen—"

"True enough. But yesterday a shipment of something else, something that doesn't belong on the refinery, was misdelivered. It's on that pallet over there, waiting to be returned. Only, if the tank goes up, it'll combine with what's in those barrels into a toxic disaster. The way the prevailing winds are blowing, I'd say the whole of Jersey City would be asphyxiated."

"Bill! You've got to do something!" I almost yelled it out, then realized where we were. "Why didn't you just call the plant and tell them they had a problem?"

"Didn't your mother ever tell you—if you want something done right, you'd better do it yourself?"

That was the whole lesson right there, but I didn't grasp it. Even after the episode with Miss Fonseca and the car bomb in front of the Soviet embassy, I was still ready to let someone else, anyone else, even an eighty-year-old Eskimo woman, do the job.

"Up there, Dexter. You've only got to turn the valve six inches counterclockwise, but you'd better hurry," Miss Betty prompted me.

Sure—what did they care? They could fly away, or dematerialize. Mere physical explosion of matter into energy couldn't harm beings such as them.

Thinking about it afterward, I never would have entered the cylinder that encased the ladder up the side of that tank... never would have climbed two hundred slippery metal rungs, inevitably coated with a light slick of oil residue... I never would have climbed out on the narrow catwalk that girded the tank—and never, ever, could I have found the strength to brace myself in the high dark and heave to on the wheel of the valve while the wind grabbed at my pantlegs and whipped my hair and the ground below swayed dizzily in my vision—never could I have done those things if I hadn't been bolstered by a growing belief that the Thirty-Six were divinely inspired, and that, like them, I was on a mission from God or *Shekhina* or Universal Mind or whatever you choose to call It. Ever so dimly, in the reflected brilliance of the Thirty-Six, I too caught a faint glimmer of His shining appearance.

31

Anarchy in the Vegetable Kingdom

With fresh insight, I resumed the hunt anew. It was about this time that things began to degenerate rapidly in the world at large. First an ill-conceived and poorly executed genetic engineering experiment on a strawberry field in the state of Washington went out of control—quietly, like a psychopath, with homicidal results.

It began innocently enough as a test of a new mutating gene. In theory, when grafted onto a plant, this gene would examine growth conditions for, say, strawberries, on its own, then mutate in one generation to the optimal shape, size, root structure, acid balance, and photosynthetic level for its environment. In other words, give the plant one generation, and it would produce the perfect seed for its species. That was the theory.

What happened in fact was that this new gene began to

166

mutate, all right, but without regard to remaining a strawberry. It mutated anywhere it could leap, be blown on the wind, rub off on, be eaten and transmitted. Well, you get the idea. Fortunately its rampant mutation was confined to the plant world. Within a month, the former agricultural cornucopia of Washington was a quarantined state whose only exports were fantastic rumors of incredibly fast-growing, thorny-spiked and mobile man-eating vines and other hideous new creations in the vegetable kingdom.

I sat in my office above Times Square and tried to think of where to search next. Washington State was out, of course, and I'd never eat a Willamette Valley apple again, but that left the rest of the planet.

Short of opening an atlas at random, I was running out of inspiration and receiving none from the Thirty-Sixers. I was nearly desperate when a second catastrophe struck, further limiting the range of my pursuit.

This too was a human-engineered tragedy. A foul-up at a virus-testing lab in France resulted in the release of a vaccine that gave those inoculated a virulent form of the disease it was supposed to prevent.

The virus spread like a medieval plague through Europe. Travel to and from the United States was banned except for the most pressing exigencies. Mine was the most pressing of all, but I couldn't tell it to the Department of State—they'd have me in the gooney colony in no time.

Now it was certain—either I would find him or her in America, or not at all. I didn't need grotesque reminders such as the new plague or the riotous plants of Washington to remember that a deadline approached for which there would be no extension, no dispensation, no relief.

32

All Blessings Flow (Very Large Array)

The whole idea is wacky, so why not a schizo Thirty-Sixo? I asked myself. To see this world continuously through innocent eyes could drive one insane. I decided to pick a hospital at random, avoiding Bellevue or any other place in the city as too implausible, and settled instead for the Poughkeepsie *Yellow Pages*, picked arbitrarily from my invaluable collection of phone books, the Bibles of the talent business.

No problem. There was half a column of loony bins to choose from. I shut my eyes and let my fingers do the walking to a listing for the Poughkeepsie Institute for Emotional Regenesis, a progressive little place whose advertising motto intrigued me: "When all else fails, come to us." It seemed appropriate—that was my current state of affairs—I'd come to them.

That afternoon I drove up the Taconic State Parkway into the farm country of the Hudson River valley, lovely variegated rolling hills only occasionally blighted by industrial ghettos such as Poughkeepsie. Fortunately, the institute was located away from the river and the depressed postindustrial wastelands in a pleasant side valley about to be overrun by tract housing, as the feasible commute from New York City was stretched to new limits by high-speed trains. A mellow stream feeding into the Hudson had long ago created the idyllic setting for the Institute, a few acres of sloping meadow on its banks.

"You've come to the right place," Dr. Trent, the hospital administrator, told me with an unpleasant smile. His pinched face was waxy and shiny and his flaxen locks, pasted smooth against his scalp, looked like a latex imitation of human hair. If I wasn't insane, looking at his goggle eyes behind those incredibly thick bifocals might send me over the edge. "We've got two would-be Hitlers, a Napoleon, even a history buff who thinks he's Charlemagne—"

"That's not quite it, Trent." I'd gotten in to see him by posing as a possible benefactor. "What we want are people whose spiritual bent has led them astray—"

"We've got two Jesus Christs and a Pope John the Twenty-third," Trent offered hopefully.

"Yes, I'll see them. Who else?" I asked, hoping to get my foot further in the door, but Trent objected when I mentioned personal interviews with his patients.

"Just a moment, Dr. Sinister." (Okay, I gave him a false impression, but time was short and my cause was just.) "Why do you need to see these people? Take my word for it—they need all the help they can get."

"I'm sorry," I insisted, hoping that the lure of grant dollars would overwhelm Trent's caution, "but I cannot authorize any funding without face-to-face contact with the recipients of our aid."

Trent wrestled with it for a minute; avarice won out. "All right," he muttered without much enthusiasm. "There's the three I mentioned, and then there's Miss Doe, you should see her."

"Doe?" I asked.

"Jane Doe—we don't know her real name."

"Who does she think she is?"

"Mr. Clean," Trent responded vaguely. I didn't know if he meant the bald fellow with the earring who pitched pine-scented cleaning fluid or some other Mr. Clean, and I was confused by the gender reference.

"Can we see her first?" I asked.

"You mean, right now?" Trent asked in surprise.

"Yes."

"Well, all right," Trent agreed reluctantly. "Come this way. The patients' quarters are in a separate facility," Trent said and removed from a belt clip an enormous ring of keys that immediately made me think of the jailers in asylums of old.

Jane Doe's room was decorated with rainbows, hundreds of rainbows of every size, some made of cloth, some of paper, some of ceramic, some of metal. The sight reminded me of bored housewives who collected figurines of owls or frogs or Hummels in a vain and desperate effort to put some variety and color into their lives.

Several rainbow mobiles blocked my initial view of Jane Doe. She was seated on her hospital bed, a standard heavy-metal job enlivened by a rainbow quilt of elaborate design, each patch a tiny mirror of the greater motif, so that the whole was a rainbow of rainbows.

I ducked under the motionless mobiles and stopped, caught up short by the look of pain and fright in Jane Doe's eyes.

"I'm not going to hurt you," I said soothingly, realizing at once that this was probably the last thing a trained therapist would say, and wondering if Trent, hovering by my right shoulder, was as astounded as Jane Doe seemed to be.

"You haven't got the quacks fight right!" Jane said, and it sounded like perfect sense until you thought about it.

"Who are you?" I asked, since she had obviously had a name before Jane Doe. Again, I could feel Trent's amazement at the absurd lack of tact in my handling of the patient, but I was determined to barrel ahead until I found out what I wanted to know or was thrown out on my earhole.

"A voice crying in the wilderness! Great soul machine, internal compulsion engine. Plasma-blaster, sine-wave master."

The woman was insane. What did I expect? I looked at Trent, who was eyeing me with a mixture of exasperation and suspicion that would have been comical if I hadn't been so pressed for time. I tried one more time for contact with this lost soul, this fragile, battered-looking woman, middle-aged yet more ravaged than my trio of spinsters, trapped in who knew what private hell, self-induced or brought on by the cruelty of others, who knew?

"Velma, Lillian, and Agatha sent me."

At this Jane Doe sat bolt upright. "I began to see that blessings flow like radio waves, they flowed through walls, through solid matter, nothing could stop them."

"Yes?" I said, to encourage her, with a dim, grievous supposition forming in my head.

She began to lecture the two of us as if a college professor, which she might have been, for all they knew at the Poughkeepsie Institute for Emotional Regenesis. "On the plains of Saint Augustin in eastern Arizona, the National Radio Astronomers group has planted a field of listening devices—tilted, white martini glasses—aimed at the sky in a Very Large Array. Do you know what they wait for?"

"No," I said dumbly.

"Blessings from above! Blessings from above!"

"How do you know so much about this?" I asked.

Her answer was nearly lucid: "It's in the waves. Phased Array, Very Large Array, Array of Arrays. Hooray!"

Somewhere within that shattered psyche was the person I sought. Somehow, I thought, I had to get through to her. Then she did it for me.

"What were the names of those friends of yours?" Jane Doe asked me again, and behind the goofily crossed eyes I could see a brilliant intellect at work, the wires crossed and sparking, to be sure, but still making wild connections of logic.

"Velma, Lillian, and Agatha."

"VLA. Very Large Array. Do they send beams of blessings?"

"Indeed they do." I started to cry. My search was over. In a home for the deranged I had found the last of the holy Thirty-Six.

Trent tugged at my sleeve, wondering what in the name of heaven had come over me, and I suspected that I was about to lose my cover, but I didn't care. I'd found them. I'd found them all!

"Come, Miss Jane Doe, or whatever your name is, your friends await you."

"Beam me up, Scotty." She was the dotty one, but it didn't matter. We started to walk out together.

"Just where do you think you're going?" Trent wanted to know.

"This woman has an appointment with destiny," I answered matter-of-factly.

That's when they slapped restraints on both of us.

33

The View from the Ninth Floor

Now we entered a new phase of the array, to use Jane Doe's analogy. The Thirty-Six would have to find us, because we weren't going anywhere.

I have a natural aversion to being confined. The crisscrossing sleeves of the restraint jacket were bound disturbingly tight around me, forcing me into a permanent hug of myself. It was very uncomfortable.

They—Trent's hospital workers, burly Teamster types who trained on the Nautilus in the employees' quarters during off hours and took unnatural pleasure in their work —had taken Jane off somewhere and put me in a padded cell. I kid you not, but I admit I was bouncing off the walls a bit, mostly with joy at having completed (I thought) my task—but also careening around in anger and frustration at being detained at the very minute I should be plowing toward the city with Ms. Doe.

After a couple of hours of fruitless cursing I slumped down, lying on one side and then the other to relieve the constant pressure of the laced-up embrace in which I held myself. There was no window in this inner room, and after I slept for a couple of stretches, I began to lose my sense of time.

The second time I woke, my mouth was dry and I was hungry. I might have slept through a night but I couldn't be sure. I called out, less a word than a loud groan, and in a minute or so the security man opened a slot and peered in.

"You gonna quiet down now?" he asked.

"No problem," I said. "I'm thirsty and hungry and I have to go the the john."

"All right, turn around."

I did as I was told and he unlaced me. My tortured shoulder muscles begged for a good massage, but instead the male nurse shoved me into the hall and down a corridor to the men's room and stood guard outside. When I came out, he escorted me back to my cell but didn't put the jacket back on, thank God.

A few minutes later, a tray of food arrived—a stainless-steel tray with molded separators between the servings, like a solid metal TV-dinner tray, filled with traditional institution food: sliced turkey in gravy, mashed potatoes, peas and carrots, apple cobbler. The utensils were curiously blunted affairs, flat and dull, with the shortest tines I'd ever seen on a fork.

An hour after that, I was brought again to Trent's offices, this time in the loose cotton pajamas of one of his inmates. He sat behind his desk as before, but our roles were vastly different now.

"Where's Jane Doe?" I asked.

"Back in her room, where she belongs. You upset her

greatly, Mr. Sinister. I've been through your wallet, you might as well know. I know who you are. What puzzles me is why a talent agent would have any interest in megalomania."

I wondered how I was going to convince a psychologist of the reality of my pursuit.

"She seemed okay to me. Did you ask her what she thought of my being here?"

"Yes. She said you were a scout. What did she mean by that?"

I took a deep breath and attempted to tell my story to Dr. Trent; though at times the disbelieving look in his eye discouraged me, I plunged on, through the episode with the pigeons at the Statue of Liberty and Bill Grebec's epic flight and right up until I realized that Jane Doe was one of them.

"Jane Doe is going to help save the world?" Trent asked.

I saw how absurd it must all look from his point of view. He probably figured I'd gone off the deep end, as had so many New Yorkers, driven mad by the grinding pace and the hellish environment.

"That's right," I said wearily. Obviously he was not won over.

"She is barely continent, Mr. Sinister. While she has the intellect of an academic, she also has the social graces of a three-year-old. How do you explain that?"

"I can't. I don't know what's happened to her. All I know is that she's the last of the Thirty-Six, and she needs to join the other thirty-five now."

"Yes, this conspiracy you keep coming back to. Have you gone to the police with your story?"

"Would you?" I asked. "They'd be less likely to believe me than you are. For some reason I was chosen as the go-between. I didn't ask to do this, but I've done the best job I can, and now it's finished; Jane was the last, and she's due in the Big Apple right away. You've got to help me, Doctor."

"Oh, I will, Sinister. It may take months or years, and many sessions, but I'll rid you of these fantasies of yours."

"You don't believe me."

"I believe that you believe you, and that Jane Doe believes you. More than that I cannot say."

"Don't I get one phone call? I mean, you can't commit me without contact with the outside world."

"We're not barbarians here, Sinister. Call anyone you like. And no one is committing you; we merely had to restrain you when you tried to leave with one of our patients. If you want to walk out right now, that's fine; but Jane Doe is our ward, and she stays."

I phoned my office but got my own answering machine. Then I called Lola Corolla.

"Lola, it's me, Dexter."

"Well, where have you been? Still chasing moonbeams?"

"I'm in an insane asylum in Poughkeepsie."

"Good for you."

"You've got to come here and help me, Lola."

"Not on your life, pal. The last time I followed you somewhere I was dive-bombed by pigeons at the Statue of Liberty, and you tried to tell me it was your holy friends, in the bodies of mindless birds, for crying out loud. I should have had you put away myself."

"Lola. Babe. Remember when I promised you that you could meet them?"

"Yeah, and the tent was gone, and pigeons don't count."

"This time I've found the last of them. She's a fascinating woman, Lola. I really think you'd like her."

"One of the nut cases?"

"Well, yes," I had to admit.

"See ya 'round, Dex. Maybe you should take a couple of

weeks, go to Hawaii or somewhere—that is, if they'll let you out."

How could I explain to Lola that I'd recently been to the South Pacific and brought back a Just Man from Tonga? I'd only sink deeper in the muck. I gave up.

"Nice talking to you, Lola."

I started to hang up, but as I did so, I heard her faint voice through the receiver. I brought the phone back up to my ear.

"Dex?"

"What is it?"

"Dex!" There was a breathless, excited quality to her voice.

I didn't know what was going on at the other end of the line. "Lola, what's wrong?"

"Dexter!"

"That's my name."

"Is one of your friends a small Asian man, and another a big, gawky fellow who looks like—like a loon?"

"That's the item," I said.

"They just appeared on my balcony."

"But Lola, you live on the ninth floor."

"Don't you think I know that?"

I heard Lola's phone drop as she rushed to the balcony window, then she came back.

"There's a whole flock of them out there, Dexter."

"Pigeons?" I asked innocently.

"People! A little Jewish boy, a guy in farmer's overalls, three old ladies—they're waving at me! Beckoning, like they want me to follow! I can't fly, Dexter!"

Now I was truly concerned. Was Lola cracking up?

"I can't believe this!" I heard her say, then there was the sound of the phone dropping again. I could picture it dangling against the refrigerator door in Lola's kitchen—that's where she kept it, on top of the fridge.

A blood-stopping scream emanated from the tiny speaker inside the telephone. Trent looked up sharply from the medical journal he was reading while I borrowed his phone. Very far off I could hear the sound of approaching police sirens on the streets of New York.

34

The Meeting Comes to Order

Lola showed up a couple of hours later. I was pacing in Trent's anteroom when she came running in, looking as if she'd jogged all the way from Manhattan. I jumped up and hugged her.

"Lola! What was that all about on the phone? You want to give me a heart attack or something?"

"You?" She pushed me away from her. Her blue eyes sparkled with fury and her black hair flew as she shook her head. "What about me? First your friends show up outside my balcony and scare me half to death, then they lure me off with them. I step off the balcony and start falling, and if Bill Grebec hadn't swooped down and caught me, I'd be a *Post* headline right now."

"Charming man, isn't he?" I asked, beaming with delight that Lola had now had the pleasure of a meeting with the Thirty-Six.

"They're all charming, Dexter. I'm honored. They're also all outside."

"Where?" I said, excited that they were all together now, or nearly so.

She led me to the window, which looked out over the pleasant grounds of the institute. "Roosting over there in that Dutch elm. See them?" She pointed to a flock of sparrows, flitting and whirling among the broad branches of a lone spreading elm on the lawn across the driveway.

"Don't talk too loud like that, Lola," I said, gesturing toward the closed door to the administrator's office, "or Trent will have you put away, too."

"I'm sorry I didn't believe you at first, Dexter, but you have to admit it's fantastic, bizarre, improbable—"

"Yeah!" I said. "Isn't it great?"

Lola slumped into one of the waiting-room chairs. "I'm exhausted. Lock me away. After what I've seen it doesn't matter."

"Did they say where they wanted to have the meeting?" I asked.

"Yes, in fact they did. I got a laugh out of it." Lola was coming around, she just needed a few minutes to catch her breath. It was her first flight, after all.

"Where? The Statue of Liberty again? Independence Hall in Philadelphia? On the steps of the Supreme Court in Washington?"

"Yankee Stadium."

"What?"

"Yeah, and you know what else? They've already picked a date."

"Oh, no. When?"

"Tomorrow."

I made some fast mental calculations, based on a quick

reading of the *Post* the previous morning, which seemed so long ago. Thanks be to heaven, the Yankees were on a road trip, their early September swing through the western division cities. The place would be empty.

"All right. But we still have to get Jane Doe out of here."

"Agatha said for me to tell you they'd take care of that. They gave me one more message for you. I hope you don't take this wrong, Dexter."

"Lay it on me."

"They said—'Tell him to get his case prepared'—do you know what that means?"

"No . . . at least I hope not." But deep down I knew.

Trent saw me off, shaking his head in disappointment that I wouldn't consider a stay in his sanatorium, but satisfied that I was no longer a threat to the safety and security of Jane Doe. At midnight that night, Jane flew freely through the window of her room into the enchanted light of the harvest moon, three times circling the place that had been her prison for eleven years, then settling in with the flock to wait for the cold dawn and the flight to the Bronx.

At the morning bed check, Jane Doe was discovered missing. Trent notified the authorities and gave them my driver's license number and a full description, which he'd copied when he rifled my wallet. Within the hour there was an all-points bulletin out for me.

Lola and I had driven back to the city that night and separated, agreeing to meet at the stadium the next day at noon. I went home to my apartment in Far Rockaway for the first time in weeks, or so it seemed, and flopped out on the living-room couch for a few hours. Just before sunset I woke up and wandered down to the beach to think about it all.

When I returned from my walk, I saw that my front door

was open, and a policeman was guarding it. I spent the
night in a motel under the name of John Smith.

I was wrong about one big detail. I knew it as soon as I
got on the A train that morning and saw all the caps and
pennants and coolers, but I refused to believe it until I got
off at 155th Street with fifty thousand others on their way
to the ballpark. The Yanks were in town. I'd miscalculated
or read the paper wrong.

What the Thirty-Six had in mind I did not know. Perhaps
they wanted witnesses. I'd arranged to meet Lola on a
streetcorner. We bought tickets in the bleachers and settled
onto the bench seats behind the centerfield fence. We were
way back, beyond the monuments of Ruth, Gehrig, and
Miller Huggins, over five hundred feet from home plate,
among the bleacher bums, the rowdy, exuberant, hard-core
drinking, doping partisans.

The visiting team was taking batting practice. Everything looked normal to me, right up through the singing of
the national anthem. Then a strange silence descended over
the stadium. This was the moment when the home team
was supposed to trot out onto the field, those inimitable
pinstripes of legend. No Yankees appeared from the first-
base dugout.

The public-address system boomed to life again: "Ladies
and gentlemen, we have an announcement. There will be
no baseball game today—"

A chorus of boos, particularly loud from the section
where we sat, greeted that statement. *It's started*, I
thought, and Lola clenched my hand tightly in hers.

"Instead," continued the voice on the PA, "we present a
spectacle entitled 'The Judgment of the World by the
Thirty-Six.' You are all invited to stay and witness this
event. Here they come now."

On cue, a flock of the everpresent Yankee Stadium pigeons began an aerial pageant that brought them closer and

closer to second base, where they soon landed and instanta-
neously turned into their human forms. The crowd, which
had been milling about, some heading for the exits and
others watching the curious flight of the pigeons, suddenly
quieted at the sight of this transformation.

"Now that we have your attention," the unseen spokes-
man continued, "please remain seated while we call the
meeting to order and summon the first witness."

Why the security guards weren't breaking in the doors of
the public-address announcer's booth, I don't know. Probably they were as stunned as any of us. Then my name was
called.

"Dexter Sinister, please come forward."

Like most every little kid who grew up in New York, I'd
had fantasies of stepping onto the hallowed stadium turf—
but in pinstripes, not as the sacrificial lamb.

35

The Cry of Abraham

Had I sold out my people without knowing it? These Thirty-Six, how much did I know about them except what they'd told me? Had I become so involved in the quest for them that I'd lost sight of what they had repeatedly warned me would be the result of their meeting: a judgment?

I didn't want to leave Lola in the bleachers by herself; so we walked together along the tunnel behind the grandstands until we reached a place beyond first base where we could pass down an aisle between boxes to field level.

I left Lola standing at the gate and stepped gingerly onto the springy grass. There were 55,456 pairs of eyes watching me cross the first-base line, careful not to step on it, and tread slowly, as one being led to the guillotine or hanging platform, to the center of the diamond. The Thirty-Six had arranged themselves in a circle, its diameter extending from the back of the pitcher's mound to the out-field grass, with second base as its center.

The PA system rumbled to life again: "The individual you see entering the field of play is Dexter Sinister, who helped us immeasurably by bringing us all together today. How about a nice round of applause for him, what do you say?"

The crowd remained silent, perhaps aware that they were in the presence of the holy.

I went around the circle, shaking hands with each of the Thirty-Six, some of whom I had never met, others such as Betty and Na'huatl, Velma, Lillian, and Agatha, whom I embraced like old friends. Mr. Chin gestured that I stand at second. The ghosts of Yankees past filed in visions before my eyes. I trotted to my position.

"What we decide today is no more and no less than the fate of the world. If we cease our virtuous contribution, the world will not end tomorrow, or the next day, but soon enough. It will slide—or rather, continue its slide—into the abyss. If, on the other hand, you, Dexter, can convince us that the world is redeemable, in your person, then we will redouble our endeavors, take up the struggle with re-newed vigor, and if any should ask us how many more times we will forgive the world, we will say not seven times but seventy times seven."

"I—I am not worthy of this honor—" I stuttered, fearful and doubtful. My words boomed over the PA, though I wore no wireless microphone.

"Nonetheless, Dexter, there will be a judgment. But first, you will be given the chance to defend humanity, by offering your own life story as testament of the worth of the world."

"Me? Oh, no! Not me, I'm just an ordinary guy. I've got hangups and secret bad desires and vindictiveness, pettiness, all the little faults of any human being—" I stopped, realizing I was only digging myself in deeper.

"You may call witnesses in your defense, and you may start by giving a deposition, if you like."

The tension in Yankee Stadium was like the seventh game of the World Series, two outs in the bottom of the ninth, one run down, bases loaded, full count, and I'm up. Naked. Without a bat.

"Wait!" I cried. "If I can't convince you, are you going to kill all the good, innocent people along with the sinners?"

"Ah, the cry of Abraham. 'Wilt thou also destroy the righteous with the wicked?'" The voice commanded, "Begin!"

36

Dexter Sinister,
This Is Your Life

After collecting my thoughts desperately, I started, and the sellout crowd that had come for baseball began to fidget and squirm as I launched into my life story.

"I was born in Canarsie. My grandfather was an Italian immigrant, Renato Sinestra, to whom somebody gave the bad advice that he should anglicize his name, hence Sinister. My father was a small businessman, he had a *groceria* in Canarsie, right across the street from the old Canarsie subway line, and he met my mother when they were both aspiring vaudevillian dancers, and I guess that's where I got the bug. I still have pictures of them in matching cowboy and cowgirl costumes, a couple of Brooklyn dudes kicking up their heels in some amateur-night contest.

"I went to PS Sixty-five and Fiorello La Guardia High School in Brooklyn; NYU; a couple of years' service be-

tween wars in the early sixties; I'm forty-five years old—
never been married," I trailed off, running out of steam.
The Thirty-Six stood about me in a circle, watchful, judg-
mental. I tried to pick up the pace.

"I got lucky on the market in the late sixties and haven't
had to work since; so I have two hobbies: one the variety
business, some of you have been there," I said, addressing
the silent Thirty-Six, and momentarily forgetting the restless crowd; "the other my penchant for going around to
spiritualist events and seeing who's running what scam and
what's real and what isn't, which is how I got into my
current predicament."

The sporting crowd, though still dazzled by the first
magical appearance of the Thirty-Six, was beginning to tire
of listening to my uneventful recitation. The beer and ice
cream vendors had begun, timidly at first, and then with
increasing boldness, to hawk their wares again, and a few
beach balls were sailing over the heads of spectators in the
right field grandstand. The visiting team's mascot, a
human-sized chicken, cavorted on his club's dugout roof.
The Yankees don't have a mascot—too undignified. From
the stands came the first yell: "Play ball!" Pretty soon there
was some serious foot-stomping and hand-clapping going
on.

A chorus of boos and Bronx cheers greeted my next
words: "I don't know for sure who these people are, surrounding me, but I know that they have great powers and
mighty intentions—and I know that there'll be no more
baseball today—"

I had to stop. Things were getting out of hand. I appealed to Mr. Chin for help, but he stared at me impas-
sively. I was on my own.

Someone in the crowd threw the first piece of rotten
fruit, and a hail of beer cups, seat cushions, beach balls,
and other junk followed until the playing surface was lit-

tered with the disposable crap the crowd would have left beneath their seats anyway. Still the Thirty-Six remained in circular formation around me, facing inward on me. A well-thrown water-balloon broke against my head, drenching me. I was knocked backward by it and stumbled over second base and fell down. A great hoot resounded in the stadium, as fifty-thousand-plus laughed at my misfortune. If this was intended to be a defense of human nature for the discerning, considering eyes of the Thirty-Six, things had not gotten off to a good start.

Then, I don't know what I was thinking of, I decided to call Lola out to be a character witness for me. I gestured for her to join me out there, and, spirited adventuress that she was, she immediately opened the gate to the field and started out. This was a bad idea for at least two reasons: first, it gave the rowdies in the centerfield bleachers the chance to show off their loudest wolf whistles while Lola strode across the field in a tight black sweater and black jeans, and second, I wasn't sure Lola could say anything positive on my behalf. Our relationship was a rocky one at best.

"This is my friend Lola Corolla," I introduced her to more whistles and catcalls, "who will say a few words about what kind of person I am. Lola—"

"Hello, everybody." Lola waved, enjoying her moment in the sun.

I could understand. How many times have you had a captive audience of fifty thousand?

"I've known Dexter Sinister for seven years now, and I know him to be a good, thoughtful, kind, considerate human being, though he doesn't call me enough, and sometimes he's a little flighty."

Flighty. What a funny word to use in the context, ringed as we were by the flightiest set of characters I'd ever encountered. I'm not flighty.

But Lola continued: "Until yesterday I didn't believe his wild story, but then I had an experience like the one you all saw just a few minutes ago. This isn't any vaudeville magic here, this is the real thing. Perhaps we ought to sit quietly and listen. I'm afraid of what will happen if we don't."

Lola, bless her heart, had restored a semblance of order to the day. The crowd quieted, and Lola sauntered back to the stands.

But I had run out of things to say about myself, and Lola was my only witness. How could I continue? Suddenly the giant video screen came up with images from my childhood, while period music played over the loudspeakers. Television! Now that was something the crowd could relate to. They settled back and watched with interest as scenes from my life that were never filmed were somehow projected onto the screen.

There I was at two, throwing a football with my left hand. There I was in my pedal automobile, the tiny terror of the neighborhood.

A few flashing scenes from elementary school, a high school prom dance, and suddenly there was young Dexter in military uniform, a rifle in hand, practicing army drills.

"I wasn't any good," I said in my own defense as the film ran, but nobody paid any attention. "They made me a clerk typist on Governors Island."

The minimovie finished up with a compilation of my experiences in finding the Thirty-Six. The audience treated these scenes as comedy and laughed uproariously when I appeared in hunting gear in Alaska and immediately afterward in a Hawaiian print shirt in Tonga.

As the last frames rolled up, the lights suddenly came on in the stadium, though it was still only early afternoon. The additional glow provided by the high-intensity carbon arc lamps lent an otherworldly cast to the unnatural green of the grass and made everything stand out in vivid contrast against it.

"Have you anything else to say?" I was asked.

"No."

"Very well. Now we will hear from the opposition."

I didn't know what was meant until the video screen exploded into a kind of berserk Movietone Newsreel of current events, featuring a long-running Middle East conflict, followed by the numerous disasters, repressions, oppressions, dissensions, and chaos that was the general state of the world. The Yankee Stadium crowd was now fully enthralled. This was their steady diet, something they could understand better than the Thirty-Six strangers holding hands around second base, or an ordinary New Yorker telling them about his boring life. Scene after scene of brutalizing violence bore heavy evidence of man's inhumanity to his fellow man, to nature, to anything that stood in his way.

My pitiful life looked insignificant against the grandly bloody picture painted by these astounding clips. Taken together, they constituted an indictment. Did the assembled audience comprehend the seriousness of the presentation? Did they still want baseball? Would they still be trying to get drunk in Yankee Stadium the day the plague or fire or flood swept over them?

37

Ascension

After the video carnage, there was an uneasy stir among the baseball patrons. Perhaps the spell was wearing off, I don't know; but a few people began to edge toward the exits. Soon there would have been a mad rush if the Thirty-Six hadn't at that moment begun to move together toward me. That stilled the crowd. The Thirty-Six were closing around me. I felt like the object of a stoning, but they only wanted to touch me and lift me gently up. I waved toward Lola, but pretty soon we were at the level of the light stanchions and climbing, and I lost sight of her.

The crowd was now on its feet and roaring. People had entirely forgotten about baseball and were thoroughly satisfied with the day's entertainment—two videos sandwiched between two of the finest magic tricks ever witnessed. We ascended to a standing ovation.

We rose straight up, banked left to stay out of the glide path of incoming flights to Kennedy, then up and up we went, until the air thinned out and I began to shiver from the cold and pant for lack of oxygen. Then we descended onto a mighty billowing thunderhead; and into its stormy head we flew and stopped. Here in this cathedral of clouds, I knew, the final judgment would take place.

Within the thunderhead was a room—well, not so much a room as a space—where the Thirty-Six had arrayed themselves like urns in the niches of a vast columbarium in two long rows. I had been placed on a pillowy platform at one end of this hall of mist.

"Aren't you afraid a jet will come ripping through here?" I asked.

"Oh, stuff and nonsense," Agatha replied from her position not far from me.

"Why haven't I frozen or suffocated?" I asked, but then I realized that with all their other powers, sustaining me inside an artificial cloud room was child's play. I accepted it and tried to relax. I might have thought I was dreaming the whole thing in my bed in Far Rockaway, except that every few minutes I caught a glimpse of the sun glinting off the back of a passing airliner, from above.

38

The Feather of Truth

The Thirty-Six began to sing. A celestial choir it was, and the music heavenly. I didn't recognize the tune, but I knew the composer, beyond any doubt. Those passages of sheer exultation and despair could only have come from the mind and pen of one man: Simon Declaville. It was divine, even though they sang a cappella, which was not Mr. Declaville's specialty—he was an instrumentalist.

When the hymn ended, a Thirty-Sixer I had not met before came forward. As soon as he spoke, I recognized the announcer's voice from Yankee Stadium.

"Welcome to the Hall of Double Justice, Dexter Sinister."

"Who are you?"

"A member of the group. You did not have to find me. I

heard the call and came to the tent the evening you were away."

"Ahhh." Really, I was speechless. The basso voice belonged to a tall, portly black man, balding with a halo of frizzy gray hair, who looked like he could be deacon in a Baptist church, a plumber or carpenter, maybe, with big calloused hands and a friendly workman's smile. He was wearing painters pants and a blue workshirt.

"What happens now?" I wanted to know.

From somewhere, the man, who hadn't told me his name, produced a scale, an old-fashioned penny-weight scale, with two small hoppers on chains counterbalancing each other off the T-bar of a center pole. In old-time candy and dry-goods stores, they used to weigh out merchandise on those things, and the blindfolded figure of Justice is seen carrying a representation of one in statues. What was I thinking? This was *it!*

"What is your name?" I asked the black man, because the crazy thought went through my head that I had the right to know my accusers, though this was not a court of law and I wasn't on trial for anything, and there was nothing at stake except maybe the fate of the world.

"Frank Wilson. Ordinary man, ordinary name. I was a welder until a few months ago. Made this on the side," he said, referring to the plain and simple balance he held in his hand. "Know what it's for, Dexter Sinister?"

"Afraid I don't," I replied. I was afraid and I didn't know.

"An ancient ritual. We take your life, all your deeds, good and bad, all the things you've ever said, thought, and done, and we put them on this side of the scale," he explained, gesturing to the left-hand side. Though nothing appeared in the pan, the scale shifted perceptibly, as an invisible weight bore it down, the weight of my sin-filled life. "Then we take this feather," and into his hand floated a tiny fluffy bit of down, "and we place it on the other side of the scale, like so. This is the feather of truth."

I watched in terror as the feather spilled lazily from his overturned hand and drifted down into the right-hand tray. It landed without a sound, without a quiver, ever so softly. The scales did not stir.

"Looks bad for the home team," I managed to say.

"Ah, but the ritual is not yet finished. Now we add to the feather of truth our loving compassion." The scales again tipped as if registering the weight of unseen items. The balance swung back to nearly even, but my life still dragged down the left-hand side, laden with regrets, omissions, commissions, moments of thoughtlessness, years of steadily falling from innocence into a crusty, selfish middle-age.

"Looks like I still come up short," I said, not understanding the meaning of it all.

"Then you must try harder, Dexter Sinister."

"I have wandered off course," I said absently, musing on the wreckage of my life.

"We have wandered off course. All of us."

"I will try harder," I said, and at my words the scale evened out so perfectly no one could have told which side was the heavier. The cloud began to glow and swirl around me. The Thirty-Six left their places, where most of them had stood at attention through the ceremony of the weighing, and paraded past me one by one, as if in farewell.

"Now comes the judgment," Lillian told me, and she patted me on the head maternally as she passed by. "Don't worry, Dexter, you've done all you could."

I didn't know what to make of that, but I couldn't think about it too much because the cloud room was disintegrating at a frightening rate, the thunderhead turning into a black rotating funnel.

You've heard of people being miraculously sucked up into the vortex of a tornado and placed down unhurt hundreds of yards, even miles away? I'll bet I'm the first person to be returned from the sky by one. I landed somewhere in New Jersey, in a cornfield that might have been Kansas. As I'd plummeted I'd seen a glimpse of the city in the distance, and I knew I hadn't traveled that far. I wandered around for a while and finally found a dirt road that led to a paved road that took me to a small town where I bought a Greyhound ticket for New York.

By nine that evening, I was back in my office. Familiar objects such as my typewriter and even the phone seemed serenely beautiful to me, a man who had just had his life torn apart, and not by a tornado. I awaited the coming judgment with fear and trepidation, and a most awful—in the old meaning of the word, that is, reverent, full of awe —sense of guilt and responsibility.

There was a message from Lola on my machine: "Dexter, thank you for the most inspiring day of my life."

I'm glad she felt that way. For myself, I was drained, physically and emotionally. I lay down on the couch that I kept not for casting purposes but so I could flop out at moments like this, and fell fast asleep.

39

The Judgment

For all his ways are judgment
Deut. 32:4

At three in the morning, the police burst into my office and yanked my arms behind my back as I slept facedown on the couch. By the time I was fully awake, I had been hauled down the stairs and into a waiting squad car. I had forgotten that I was wanted for aiding and abetting an escape from an asylum.

Somewhere, I knew, somewhere in the vaulted clouds, in the pristine air of the upper stratosphere, on the edge of space, where the world begins to show its curve, the Thirty-Six were judging the world, and they were using my life as their benchmark. I was arrested on the aid-and-abet charge, fingerprinted and mug-photoed and read my rights and brought into a small interrogation room in the Times Square precinct station, a grubby building that matched the class of criminal it housed, the pimps, purse snatchers and addicts who made up the local clientele.

Two NYPD detectives came into the room and turned the lights up bright. They must have been watching too many old television shows or something, or maybe that's the way they really do things. They crowded around me threateningly, like thugs themselves. One was tall and had garlic on his breath; the other was so nervous he chewed gum and smoked at the same time. They both wore the badge of their profession, black shiny shoes.

"All right, Sinister, tell us everything you know about the incident a month or so ago in Central Park."

I was surprised. I thought they only wanted to talk to me about Jane Doe's whereabouts. Instead they had made the connection between that event and my efforts to free Jane Doe. Perhaps yesterday's action at Yankee Stadium had opened a few eyes among the authorities. I told them all about the Thirty-Six, everything, from my first contact with them to yesterday's substitute entertainment for the ballgame, and what followed. Why not? I had nothing to lose. Obviously they had trouble believing me, but on the other hand they had fifty thousand witnesses who said I'd flown out of the ballpark escorted by a flock of angels. There was even some videotape taken by an overwrought cameraman, who on the tape is heard swearing over and over—"This isn't happening. This is not happening!"

Eventually the disgusted detectives gave up trying to get anything they considered meaningful out of me. It's funny how the truth can be a blank wall to people who aren't prepared to see it. I was allowed a phone call, to Lola, then I was taken to a solitary cell. Apparently they didn't want me mingling with the ordinary prisoners.

The Gideons had been there before me and left a Bible.

Distractedly I leafed through it until I found the chapter and verse Frank Wilson had referred to as "the cry of Abraham." Genesis 18:23. God has threatened to destroy Sodom and Gomorrah. Abraham is bargaining him down as to how many righteous men it would take to save the cities, and that's where the quote comes in. God starts at fifty but Abraham bargains him down to forty then thirty and twenty and finally knocks him down to ten, but to no avail. At the start of the next chapter the destruction has begun. But I read on to the twenty-ninth verse of the next chapter and came to this curious passage where God sort of says "Whoa! Hey! Wait a minute! Almost forgot!"

I clung to those words like a drowning man to a life buoy: "And it came to pass, when God destroyed the cities of the plain, that God remembered Abraham, and sent Lot out . . ."

Okay, so it's not the most hopeful verse. Sodom and Gomorrah are treated to the fire and brimstone, Lot's wife ends up a pillar of salt, and Lot's daughters have to conspire to sleep with him to propagate the race and found the tribes of Moab and Ammon, but at least they endure. That seemed to be the most I could hope for at this point.

The first omens of the judgment came the next morning as I lay on my mattress in my cell, listening to the drunks bitch about when they could get out of the tank.

"Hey, ain't it awful dark outside for this time of the morning?" one asked another.

"How would you know?" the other replied. "You ain't seen a sunrise since 1969."

"No, hey, take a look." The two of them were congregating by the one window in the joint, screened over with mesh but still admitting a narrow view of a slice of sky above Manhattan.

"Man, is it going to rain! Maybe we should just shut up and stay in here today."

"Naw," the other replied, "I got a date at the welfare office. Got to collect my food stamps."

A violent peal of thunder drove them back from the open window.

The drunks' inane conversation droned on. I wedged myself into the corner of my individual cell to where I could catch a glimpse of the sky from their window, and what I saw frightened me. It looked as if Manhattan had been covered by a black shroud, so dark was the sky.

Lola bailed me out that morning.

We ran for cover under the fearsomely black sky. It hadn't yet started to rain. The static-electric tension in the air was almost painful.

"Tell me where you went, what you saw!" Lola entreated me as we jogged down Forty-fourth Street toward her parked car. I had to remember that the last she saw of me I was heading toward orbit velocity without benefit of rocket or space capsule.

"Not now, Lola, not now. I'll tell you about it on the way uptown." We reached the car. "I'll drive," I said.

"Where are we going?" she asked, reasonably enough.

"Sheep Meadow. Just a hunch," I yelled over a crescendoing arpeggio of staccato thunderclaps. Strange, I hadn't seen any preceding lightning. "Anyway, we'll be able to see the sky better from there—it's more open."

"Dexter," Lola replied apprehensively, "aren't you supposed to stay away from trees and parks in thunderstorms? I'm scared."

"Honey, in this one it won't matter. Trust me."

I didn't have the heart to tell her the reason it didn't matter. We drove north and parked along Central Park West. A stream of people was leaving the park as the first oversized drops splashed down. By the time we reached Sheep Meadow it was empty of sensible people.

A few hippie types still frolicked in the rain, playing a comically amateurish game of Frisbee.

At the first mighty roar from the heavens above, however, they trotted off, staring in wonder at us. We were already soaked. We sat on the granite rock formation that rises out of the solid ground at one end of the meadow and waited for the display, which would be the grand total— the ringing up and balancing out—the weighing and the judgment of my life and the world's worth.

Pretty soon the heavens opened and the deluge struck. New York can have some pretty hellacious thunderstorms to start with, and when the thunder starts reverberating down those long concrete canyons, it can be just like being in the Southwest, where a single boom can bounce off cliff walls for minutes at a time. But this, this was more, this was unnatural, this was the work of the Thirty-Six. At times I would have sworn they were sky-writing with lightning, but I could never quite make out the letters and phrases that the fractured bolts spelled out, and maybe it was just my fevered and waterlogged imagination, for Lola and I were drenched to the skin.

Sheep Meadow danced with eerie balls of flame, St. Elmo's fire, and at one point I would have sworn that several of the burning spheres began to gyrate in the formations of five-ball juggling, but it was too hard to see through the sheeting rain.

Every few seconds the whole park was illuminated by brilliant bursts of lightning. In one of these dazzling, shattering flashes of luminosity, I thought I saw the Thirty-Six high above, like the avenging angels that visited Sodom and Gomorrah. Or perhaps they were bestowing their blessing. I could only hope.

Was it raining all over the world? Was this the beginning of the deluge, the second flood, the recurrent flood of Gilgamesh and Noah? I didn't know.

After a couple of hours, the storm blew itself out and a magnificent rainbow appeared over the skies of Central Park. Dripping wet, Lola and I wandered to the center of the meadow, eyes upward, admiring the glory of the arched spectrum of colors. I thought it was over and let my guard down. I was caught unprepared when the voice of Frank Wilson, welder, church deacon, and member of the Thirty-Six, echoed over the green: *"Now the shofar sounds again!"*

40

Solid Walls of Sound

God is gone up in shouting,
The Lord amidst the sound of the shofar.

Psalms 47:6

After the first blowing of the shofar, I went to the
dictionary and discovered that the ram's horn was blown
at the changing of the seasons, in public ceremonies, and
to signal the movements of troops on the battlefield in
attacking and retreating. It was believed that the shofar would sound from above in the last call of the Judgment.

Mr. Declaville had played once. Now his dulcet tones
sounded again, and this time they were heard 'round the
world. It was the sweetest, calmest, most penetrating note

ever played—the perfect harmonic convergence of vibration and emotion—and its effects were global.

Solid walls of sound echoed across the planet.

It was not a complete new start, only a freshening breeze, tempering and encouraging, mollifying and moderating. *For we have wandered off course,* I thought, as the sound touched me, too. I saw forgiveness and love in the eyes of Lola and everyone who passed us by—couples and old people still dreamily walking in the park under the rainbow as the shofar echoed and lingered and washed over us—and I knew that in a mirror I would see the same signs of grace in my eyes; and still the shofar blew.

It swept through the hearts of all the people of the world and blew them clean, as a fresh ocean sprite in some, as a crisp Arctic wind in others, as a warm wafting scent-laden tropical zephyr in yet others.

And the lecher's heart it made less lecherous.

And the gluttonous heart it made more finicky.

And the drunkard's heart it made more temperate.

The angry heart grew calmer.

The jealous heart became more understanding, and the wandering eye decided to stay home for a while.

The slothful heart grew energetic.

The greedy heart became more charitable.

The covetous man lost some of his craving.

The hearts of the innocent became saintlike in their purity.

And some, only a very few, the most evil, irredeemable few, it totally blew away.

41

"Maintiens le Droit"

The blowing of the shofar marked the last appearance of the Thirty-Six on Earth. At least, I never saw them again. Had they righted the ship of state? Were we back on course? A tough question, but in the next month it did seem that there were fewer muggings, rapes, and murders. On the international scene, ceasefires were reached among some long-standing combatants. Even the patrons of the subway system seemed friendlier. All of these hopeful signs were noted in the press, which had a difficult time explaining the unseen but undeniable effects of the sounding of the ram's horn, an event that would have been a headline item on par with aliens landing on the planet, if it wasn't for the obscure, mysterious nature of its workings.

Lola and I decided to marry. It was about time I settled down, and Lola had gained a new respect for me. Yes, it was safe to say that I had risen, so to speak, in stature in her eyes as a result of my participation in the episode of the Thirty-Six.

We spent a month honeymooning in Tonga as guests of Na'huatl's tribe. Those wonderful people, though they missed their leader greatly, somehow knew that he had been a key figure in the recent history of the world. They feted us with music, food, and long sessions of song.

When we came back, we both gave up our apartments and moved out of the city to a folksy gray saltbox house on Long Island, close enough for Lola to commute, and with an office for me to do business by phone, though I still wasn't sure what it was I was going to do if I gave up talent agenting.

I took frequent walks on the beach. Secretly I hoped for a return to yesteryear, searching for them. It seemed like nothing in my life would ever match the excitement of those times when I was on their trail.

I thought about social work or something. The poor we would always have with us, and not even the great second chance afforded us by the Thirty-Six could change that. The Bronx was still the Bronx, Soweto was still Soweto, Calcutta was still a black hole of human misery. But was I really a social-work kind of guy? I mean, I like the idea in theory, but when I get right down to it, I think middle-aged motherly types are better suited for it than I would be. Still, my time with them had persuaded me that I had to do something more relevant than what I had been doing before.

I went to a few interviews and came away with a sense of having confronted a system still lacking sympathy, tenderness, concern, or any of the other attributes I thought would be requirements for the job. So what was I to do?

One evening I was strolling alone on the beach when I heard a "*Pssst, pssst*" behind me. I knew who it was, but I didn't turn around right away. I wanted to savor the moment. "*Pssst!* You! It's me." Out of the corner of one eye I glimpsed the hem of a black garment. There could be no mistake. It was the rabbi again. He put his hand on my shoulder. "Shalom. Please, a word with you."

I faced him. "Thank you," I said. "Thank you."

"You are most welcome. And thank you. You did your job most admirably. However—"

"Yes?" I jumped in quickly, eager to do anything for this man who had introduced me to the Thirty-Six.

"Your task is not finished."

"It's not!" I cried with joy. "What else can I do? Just name it."

"Do you know the motto of the Royal Canadian Mounted Police?"

"'We always get our man?' Yeah, I suppose I can see how that applies to me, after all I found Thirty-Six before —" I rattled on idiotically.

The rabbi cut me off. "Not that motto, Sinister; the real, official motto: *Maintiens le droit*."

I dusted off my high school French. Of course, it wasn't that tough, you could sound it out without even knowing the language. "Maintain the right?"

"Correct."

"So?"

"That is your task, the task of all men."

"Maintain the right."

"That is it. The Thirty-Six have counterbalanced one dangerous swing of the pendulum. It is up to all of us to maintain the right, to see that such drastic oscillations do not threaten us again. Do you follow me?"

"What can I do?"

"*Maintiens le droit*."

"But where? When? How?"

"Everywhere, all the time, by whatever means possible. Nonviolently, of course."

"That's too vague for me," I said, launching into another spiel. "I need some concrete notion; I want somebody to tell me what to do." I ran on for a minute or so before I became aware that I was talking to myself.

Evening found me still pacing on the beach. We had moved far enough out on the island that the glow of New York did not dim the glory of the night sky. It was a moonless night. The stars of the Milky Way stretched like a white carpet toward heaven. The thought had come to me that these Thirty-Six were gone, somehow used up in the effort it took to preserve us. By rights, then, another, new Thirty-Six must have taken their place. By what means the succession was effected I knew not, but I was sure that the line would go on. If that was so, I would look for them, and when I found them I would ask them what to do.

But then I understood that I already had their answer: "*Maintiens le droit*." No, I must not search out the new Thirty-Six. They must remain anonymous, that their exertions might go on uninterrupted. But what was I to do?

It was Lola who gave me the idea. After about six weeks of my moping about the house, she was fed up.

"Why don't you start up the agency again?" she asked. "It's what you really love to do."

"Being a talent agent just isn't making enough of a social contribution, Lola."

"It is if you're a good talent agent, Dexter. All you can do is do your best." She was right. I could do charity events, protest concerts, telethons. There was a whole world crying out for my skills.

So I hung out the shingle again at Dexter Sinister's Variety Arts Talent Agency. If you know any good acts, give me a call. I'm in the book. The agency is doing quite well.

There have been no further visitations from the Thirty-Six. But I'll tell you this, I'm still very careful when I see rabbis on the A train, or three of any bird, insect, or animal together. And on certain Fridays now, I, who am not Jewish, go to temple just to hear them blow that crazy horn.

The WIZARD WAR CHRONICLES

An epic sword and sorcery quest series from Hugh Cook

☐ **WIZARD WAR**
(E20-700, $3.95, U.S.A.) (E20-701, $4.95, Canada)
An evil wizard has stolen a potent artifact, and it's up to a handful of noble wizards to recapture it before it works its lethal magic on the entire world.

☐ **THE QUESTING HERO:**
Wizard War Chronicles I
(E20-664, $3.95, U.S.A.) (E20-665, $4.95, Canada)
A brave young warrior goes questing for a fabled scripture, and finds himself on an adventure-filled odyssey through strange lands.

Questar
SCIENCE FICTION

POPULAR LIBRARY

 **Warner Books P.O. Box 690
New York, NY 10019**

Please send me the books I have checked. I enclose a check or money order (not cash), plus 95¢ per order and 95¢ per copy to cover postage and handling.* (Allow 4-6 weeks for delivery.)

___Please send me your free mail order catalog. (If ordering only the catalog, include a large self-addressed, stamped envelope.)

Name_____

Address_____

City _____ State _____ Zip _____
*New York and California residents add applicable sales tax.   328

From fantasy master
M. COLEMAN EASTON

☐ **SWIMMERS BENEATH THE BRIGHT**
(E20-456, $2.95, U.S.A.) (E-20-457, $3.95, Canada)
Three inhabitants of the planet Safehold must save themselves from the tyranny of alien cells.

☐ **MASTERS OF GLASS**
(E20-424, $3.50, U.S.A.) (E20-425, $4.50, Canada)
In a land where people are protected by magical glass talismans, an old glassmaker breaks with tradition to take on a female apprentice—and the two begin a quest that will test them both to their uttermost limits.

☐ **ISKIIR**
(E20-151, $3.50, U.S.A.) (E20-152, $4.50, Canada)
A young wanderer holds the power to undo the secret evil of huge black monoliths magically stalking forth to crush his city.

☐ **THE FISHERMAN'S CURSE**
(E20-332, $3.50, U.S.A.) (E20-333, $4.50, Canada)
The village of Darst is fated to fall victim to the horrible sea demon Etma...unless Kyala, the novice Vigen, can worthily wield the magic beads.

**Ⓦ Warner Books P.O. Box 690
New York, NY 10019**

POPULAR LIBRARY

Please send me the books I have checked. I enclose a check or money order (not cash), plus 95¢ per order and 95¢ per copy to cover postage and handling.* (Allow 4-6 weeks for delivery.)

___Please send me your free mail order catalog. (If ordering only the catalog, include a large self-addressed, stamped envelope.)

Name _____

Address _____

City _____ State _____ Zip _____

*New York and California residents add applicable sales tax.   318